Her heartbeat thudding Suzy lifted her lashes

She half expected to see a glint of sardonic amusement in the dark eyes looking down at her, but for once his lean face held no mockery. He had his deliberating look; the expression he wore before an important decision. She had seen it too often not to recognize it, even though this time it was combined with the unfamiliar signs that he, too, was aroused.

She knew she was flushed. She could feel the hot blood in her cheeks. But she hadn't expected to see that his color had risen. His eyes held a strange burning light, almost frightening in its intensity.

"Are you sure this is what you want, Susan?" His voice was thicker than usual.

She didn't hesitate. "Yes...."

Books by Anne Weale

ANTIGUA KISS
FLORA

HARLEQUIN PRESENTS

HARLEQUIN ROMANCES

These books may be available at your local bookseller.

For a free catalog listing all titles currently available,
send your name and address to:

Harlequin Reader Service
P.O. Box 52040, Phoenix, AZ 85072-9988
Canadian address: Stratford, Ontario N5A 6W2

ANNE WEALE

ecstasy

Harlequin Books

TORONTO • NEW YORK • LONDON
AMSTERDAM • PARIS • SYDNEY • HAMBURG
STOCKHOLM • ATHENS • TOKYO • MILAN

Harlequin Presents first edition February 1984
ISBN 0-373-10670-X

Original hardcover edition published in 1983
by Mills & Boon Limited

CHAPTER ONE

A LITTLE more than three hours after take-off from New York, the British Airways supersonic jet Concorde landed at Heathrow in England.

The first of the eighty-two passengers to leave the aircraft was a man with black hair and dark eyes who said a courteous goodbye to the stewardess who had served him with a champagne breakfast more than ten miles above the earth's surface, at a speed twice as fast as sound.

Among the many advantages of the Concorde service were that boarding and landing procedures involved none of the tedious delays which could happen on ordinary flights. Baggage reclaim and immigration formalities were made as painless as possible; and, as the majority of Concorde's passengers were top-level businessmen, most had chauffeur-driven limousines awaiting them.

For the tall man whose smiling farewell had left the pretty stewardess regretting that, although a regular passenger, he had never tried to make a date with her, leaving the airport was even quicker than for the rest of the passengers. He had crossed the Atlantic without baggage, apart from the black leather briefcase containing the papers he had studied during the latter part of the flight.

He had left New York at eight-thirty a.m. Because this was a different time zone, his driver said, 'Good evening, Mr Vyner,' as he opened the door of the gleaming black Rolls-Royce.

Vyner used the drive to central London to dictate some memoranda to a pocket recorder. His destination was the Connaught, an élite hotel in the heart of Mayfair where, for years, one of the twenty-two suites had been reserved for his exclusive use. It was his home when in London. In New York he lived at the Pierre; in Paris at the Plaza-Athénée.

At weekends he was usually a guest at a country house, château or hunting lodge where he could enjoy the pleasures of rural and domestic life without the concomitant staff problems, heavy overheads, marital tiffs and worries about their children which his hosts had to bear.

The way he travelled was typical of his whole life-style. Expensive. Luxurious. Unencumbered.

As a younger man, on his way up, he had had the reputation of being a playboy. Now, still in his thirties and securely established as a financial genius, that side of his life provided less fodder for the gossip columnists; although from time to time they would marvel at his ability to engage several beautiful women in long, harmonious relationships although each of them knew she had only a share of his affections and was unlikely to graduate from mistress to wife.

On reaching his suite, which the hotel had furnished to suit him and where the paintings and *objets d'art* were his own, Vyner switched on the television to see if he could catch a newscast.

When the picture appeared, without the sound, there were three people on the screen. One of the women was an interviewer he had seen before. The other people were unknown to him. The man's appearance was uninteresting, but something about the girl made Vyner pause before trying another channel.

She appeared to be in her middle twenties with fair hair smoothed back from a broad, intelligent forehead, a good skin and large grey eyes. If she was wearing make-up, it was only detectable in the colour of the rose-pink lipstick on her beautiful, passionate mouth.

A mouth completely at variance with the rest of her.

Except that her hair was uncovered, she looked like a nun whose order had adopted modern dress. He noted the details—white blouse, plain grey suit, grey tights, black court shoes with medium heels.

She sat like a nun, feet together, knees hidden, hands loosely clasped in her lap. She had a nun's calm expression. Not for her the sideways glance at the monitor to see how she looked to the viewers, or any of the gestures which betrayed nervous tension or selfconsciousness. He could see that her whole attention was on the middle-aged man and whatever he was telling the interviewer.

At this point Vyner realised that someone must have turned down the sound, or the set wasn't working properly. He soon found it was the latter.

As he moved to the telephone to ask for another set to be brought to his suite immediately, he continued to watch the girl in grey and to wish he were able to lip-read.

Now it was her turn to answer the interviewer's questions. Once or twice, as she did so, she smiled, her grey eyes dancing with humour; and one question made her laugh, her lovely lips parting to show attractive white teeth.

He found it impossible to believe a girl with that kind of mouth could have a religious vocation. But if she was not a nun, what was she? And why was she on television?

The answer was in all the national newspapers which he liked to see while in England and which were arranged in a neat row on a table on the other side of the room. But he didn't find that out till later and, before the replacement TV arrived, the interview was over.

In a small, old-fashioned hotel, frequented by country

parsons and members of the Women's Institute, Suzy Walker switched off the set on which she and Alix Johnson had been watching the interview recorded several hours earlier.

'You didn't seem at all nervous. Had they plied you with gin beforehand?' asked Alix, who had arrived only just in time to see the part of the programme dealing with Suzy's sudden emergence from obscurity into a brief blaze of nationwide publicity.

'They offered it, but I thought it was probably better to stay cold sober,' said Suzy, her grey suit now changed for a dress and her hair swinging loose on her shoulders instead of coiled behind her head. 'It really wasn't too much of an ordeal. I knew what she was going to ask me and I'd thought out my answers beforehand. However, enough about me. I want to hear all about you. Oh, Alix, it *is* lovely to see you. I do wish you could come home more often, or would write more often. I miss you enormously.'

The two had been friends since their schooldays and still felt a strong affection, even though fate had decreed that Suzy remain in the small Yorkshire town which was their birthplace while the other girl came south to be a nurse in one of London's famous teaching hospitals.

Alix said, 'I miss you, too. But you know how it is; I don't get on with Gerald'—her mother's second husband—'and the train fare keeps going up. I know I'm a rotten correspondent, but I seem to have so little time. If I could type, it would help. Writing letters by hand takes forever. Why don't you come to London more? Your salary is better than mine. You can afford it, and it would do you good. You ought not to be stuck in Brockthorpe—it's such a dull little town. I don't know how you can stand it.'

'Now that Dad has retired and can look after Mother, I probably shall come more often. In fact as

Mr Howard is also on the point of retiring, I'm considering changing my job. He thinks it would be a mistake for me to stay and work for his successor. He feels that, having learnt French and Spanish, I ought to find a post where I can use them.'

'He's absolutely right,' agreed Alix. 'You're wasted up there in the wilds of the North Riding, Suzy. I wonder if your being on TV this evening will bring in any interesting offers? It's a pity you didn't mention you were looking for a change of scene. I should think as 'Britain's Top Secretary' you could take your pick of any number of super jobs.'

Suzy laughed. 'You shouldn't believe all you read in the newspapers, Alix. I'm not really Britain's top secretary. That's a title invented by the Press which they give every year to whoever wins the gold medal. This year there were six hundred candidates for the private secretary's diploma, and over a hundred of us passed. I just happened to get the highest marks, but a lot of girls were close behind me, and none of us is necessarily as good a secretary as someone without the diploma but with years of practical experience. I'm starving! Let's go and eat, shall we?'

Alix who, since leaving home, had had a succession of love affairs, mostly with medical students and impoverished young doctors, was an expert on where to eat well but inexpensively. She took Suzy to an Italian restaurant where, as neither of them had a weight problem, they enjoyed large helpings of *tagliarini verdi*, a green pasta made on the premises by the proprietor and his wife, followed by home-made ices.

While they ate, Alix talked about her current and most serious romance with a doctor called Mike whom she longed to marry but couldn't bring to the point.

Listening to her, admiring her chestnut hair and tawny eyes, Suzy wondered why he was jibbing.

Could it be because he was already enjoying the privileges of marriage without its responsibilities? Alix wasn't living with him, but they had been lovers almost from the outset of their relationship. Suzy knew that her friend's mother and stepfather and her own parents would be shocked if they knew how many lovers Alix had had. Yet she wasn't a promiscuous person. It was merely that she didn't believe in the old double standard which had prevailed in their parents' youth. If she liked and was attracted by a man, she didn't see why she shouldn't sleep with him.

Suzy was never quite certain where she herself stood on that issue. She had theoretical views, but they hadn't been tested. In her early teens she had fallen in love with the boy next door. At nineteen, a virgin, she had married him. At twenty-one she had been widowed.

It had taken a long time to recover. By then all the other young men in her circle had either left Yorkshire or were married. She would have left Yorkshire herself, but for being needed at home to help care for her semi-invalid mother.

The result was, at twenty-four, she was still a widow whose experience of other men's embraces was confined to one or two unwelcome advances by the type of man who assumed that all widows must be so sex-starved they would fall into anyone's arms.

'Perhaps you ought to try not seeing Mike for a while, Alix,' she suggested. 'It might make him realise how important you are to him.'

'Or it might do exactly the reverse and make him realise how unimportant I am,' answered Alix, with a wry grimace. 'He's too damned good-looking, and also he has a private income, so he can afford to wine and dine girls more lavishly than most young medics. When he first started taking me out, we went to all the top places, and we still do, if not quite as often. But I'm pretty sure that if I broke it off, even temporarily, it wouldn't be five minutes before he'd be squiring other girls around town.'

When Suzy said nothing, she went on, 'I know what you're thinking; that, in that case, he can't really love me. But the thing is that *I* love *him*, and if I can keep things going on their present basis, maybe one day he'll feel it's time we made it official.'

To Suzy's way of thinking it was an intolerable situation. But then, a long time ago, Alix had thought she was mad to tie herself down in a youthful marriage to Chris.

It was never any use advising people. They had to use their own judgment and, if it were wrong, live with or learn from their mistakes. How her marriage would have worked out in the long run was something she would never know.

But she did know she was a different person from the starry-eyed girl who had walked up the aisle on her father's arm. Sometimes, looking back, she was appalled to remember what a frivolous young thing she had been then—never reading anything but fashion magazines, bored by her first office job, living for the evenings when Chris would take her dancing.

'You're thinking about Chris, aren't you?' Alix said gently.

Vexed with herself for allowing her thoughts to wander from her friend's problems, she nodded.

'It's three years, Suzy. He wouldn't have wanted you to go on mourning. That's another reason why you ought to leave Brockthorpe. You'll never meet anyone interesting there.'

'I know . . . and I don't grieve for Chris,' Suzy said quietly. 'There'll always be a corner of my heart which is his. But I'm ready to love someone else now.'

'Just be careful who you fall for, that's all. Living at home all this time, spending your evenings at language classes and studying for your diploma, you could easily succumb to the first attractive man who makes a set at you,' Alix warned her.

She smiled as she said it, but she wasn't altogether joking. Although Suzy was now a full member of the Institute of Qualified Private Secretaries, and a much more level-headed, well-read and mature person than she had been at nineteen, Alix suspected that, emotionally, she was dangerously vulnerable.

An unscrupulous man would make mincemeat of her; and after what she had already been through, she might not survive another trauma.

When Suzy returned to her hotel—fairly early because it had been a long, exciting day and she and Alix were seeing each other again the following evening—she was surprised to see a fold of paper in the pigeonhole above her room key. As she didn't know anyone in London except Alix, she wondered if her father had telephoned while she was out, and if anything was wrong at home.

However, when the note was given to her, she found it was a message asking her to telephone the spokesman for the London Chamber of Commerce and Industry who had been on television with her.

He had been asked to appear to give the history of the diploma she had won, and to explain that the candidates were not only required to have high speeds in shorthand and typing but had to report a filmed conference, and be interviewed by a panel of senior businessmen.

Wondering why he should want her to ring him 'as a matter of urgency', she went up to her room and dialled his number.

'Ah, Mrs Walker, good evening,' he said, when he answered the phone. 'Am I right in thinking that you aren't leaving London until the day after tomorrow?'

'Yes, that's right, Mr Cooper. Tomorrow I'm going

to do some sightseeing and shopping, and in the evening I'm going to the theatre.'

'I see. Well, most of the stores and places of interest don't open before half past nine or ten, so having breakfast with Mr Vyner shouldn't interfere with your arrangements.' He laughed, as if he had said something humorous.

'Who is Mr Vyner?' she asked, assuming he must be a media man.

'Mr Wolfe Vyner, the financier.' Mr Cooper sounded as if he expected this additional information to elicit instant recognition.

But Suzy was obliged to say, 'I'm sorry, I've never heard of him. Is he one of your VIPs?'

'In the City of London and in Wall Street, Mr Vyner is generally regarded as one of the outstanding men of our time,' replied Mr Cooper. 'In little more than a decade he has built himself a commercial empire which must make him one of the richest men on either side of the Atlantic.'

His tone made her feel as if she had admitted never to having heard of John D. Rockefeller or the Rothschild dynasty.

'Goodness! Why does he want me to have breakfast with him?'

'It's the only time he can spare tomorrow. He happened to see us on television earlier this evening and he thinks you may be a suitable person to replace his present secretary. He would like you to be at his hotel at eight o'clock. Perhaps you would be good enough to ring me at the office and let me know the outcome of the interview. If he does decide to engage you, it will make an excellent news story and highlight the value of the diploma. He's staying at the Connaught Hotel, which is rather too far to walk from where you're staying. You'll need to take a taxi. The Connaught at eight o'clock. Do you want to write it down?'

'I already have,' said Suzy.

'Good: in that case it only remains to wish you luck, Mrs Walker. Don't forget to call me tomorrow. Goodnight.'

'Goodnight.'

She replaced the receiver and for several minutes sat staring at the notes she had made in her small, neat handwriting.

Wolfe Vyner. Connaught Hotel. 8 a.m.

Was he English or American? An American, presumably. For surely, if he were English and as important as Mr Cooper made out, she couldn't have failed to hear of him? The fact that he was staying at a hotel supported that conclusion.

She had read that to some Americans an English butler was a status symbol. Perhaps Mr Vyner felt an English private secretary had the same sort of cachet. It was clear now why Mr Cooper had laughed after saying that breakfast with Mr Vyner wouldn't interfere with her plans. Obviously, in his opinion the chance to breakfast with a millionaire was on a par with a summons to Buckingham Palace. Perhaps, in a way, he was right. It might be rather fun: another London adventure to describe to her family when she got home. A pity he wasn't staying somewhere more glamorous like the Ritz, the Savoy or the Dorchester. She had never heard of the Connaught.

At twenty minutes to eight the following morning, Suzy stood on the south side of Mount Street, at the junction with Carlos Place, looking at the unpretentious Edwardian red brick façade of Mr Vyner's hotel.

She had passed a rather restless night and, rising at six, had decided to walk to her appointment. The night before, when she had asked the receptionist at her hotel where the Connaught was, the girl had given her a tourist map. With this she had worked out a route which had enabled her to see something of Regent Street and Bond Street and to walk round Berkeley Square.

At this hour of the morning London was relatively deserted. She had enjoyed swinging along in the comfortable, low-heeled shoes she needed to wear for shopping and sightseeing later.

Yesterday, for the press and TV interview, she had dressed as she did for the office. Today, apart from her neatly coiled thick blonde hair, her appearance was more informal. She was wearing a camel-coloured pleated skirt, a cream open-necked shirt with a scarf knotted round her slim throat, and a camel Shetland cardigan which she could remove if the heat in the stores was too much for her.

If Mr Vyner didn't like the way she looked, it wasn't a matter of great moment, because she had already decided that she didn't want to work in America. It was too far away; too big a transition from Brockthorpe. It would be better to try working in London for a year and see how she liked that before venturing farther afield.

However, she had no scruples about going through with the interview, because it was not as if he were wasting his working time on her; and, if he did offer her the post, it would be valuable publicity for the diploma and a feather not only in her cap but of all qualified private secretaries.

As she crossed to the other side of Mount Street, intending to walk in the direction of Park Lane until it was time to enter the hotel, she noticed a tall, dark-haired man coming towards her.

His black track suit, running shoes and sweatband indicated that he had been jogging in Hyde Park. But at the moment he was walking and, as he approached, she was struck by the lithe elasticity of his long stride. At first, because of the way he moved, she thought he was younger than she; a man in his early twenties, full of energy and élan, as Chris had been.

However, as he came nearer, she realised he was somewhat older, with a deeply-tanned, raw-boned face which had something foreign about it. Not an English face. Italian, perhaps, or Greek. Except that none of the people round the Mediterranean were noted for their height, and he was as tall and long-limbed as the Scandinavians.

Before he was near enough to notice her staring at him, she looked away, pretending an interest in the buildings on the opposite side of the street, meaning to have another quick look at him as they came abreast.

Then, to her amazement, when he was a few yards away, he said, 'Good morning, Mrs Walker. I'm Wolfe Vyner.'

Suzy almost jumped out of her skin. She hadn't expected him to speak to her and, at first, she couldn't believe he was who he said he was. He couldn't be less like her preconception of an American financier.

'I think you'd find my hand rather sticky at the moment. We'll shake hands when I've taken a shower. I wasn't expecting you yet. Are you always an early arriver?' he asked, with a gesture which suggested that, instead of standing still, gaping at him, she should start retracing her steps.

Suzy pulled herself together.

'No, not usually. But I'm a stranger in London. I wasn't sure how long it would take to walk here.'

'Where are you staying?'

She felt sure the name of her hotel would mean as little to him as his had to her. She said, 'Near the British Museum.'

'It's quite a walk from Bloomsbury to here, but you're sensibly shod, I notice. Do you do much walking?'

'At the weekends, yes . . . quite a lot. I live in good walking country.'

Clearly he had a good memory. He didn't ask where that was, but said, 'I've flown over Yorkshire a few times on my way to Scotland, but I've never been there. Have you always lived there?'

'All my life. I've had two holidays in France, but that's the limit of my travels. Even the south of England is new territory to me. You've travelled a great deal, I expect?'

'I travel all the time. I like it. Too long in any one place makes me restless,' he answered. 'I'm glad to hear you don't make a habit of arriving unnecessarily early for your appointments. That's as wasteful of time as being unpunctual. What would you like for breakfast?'

'Oh . . . anything . . . whatever you're having.'

'You might not like what I'm having. What would you like?' His tone made it clear that when he asked a question he expected a precise answer.

Slightly ruffled, she named the first things which came into her head.

'Grapefruit and scrambled eggs please.'

'With tea or coffee?'

'Coffee, please.'

By this time they had reached the entrance to the hotel. As they crossed the lobby, Wolfe Vyner said good morning to one or two members of the staff. They knew him by name, which suggested that he stayed there regularly.

Expecting to have breakfast in public, Suzy thought he would ask her to wait downstairs while he went up to shower and change. When he moved in the direction of the lifts, she said uncertainly, 'Shall I wait here?'

He glanced down at her, looking faintly surprised by the question. Then, almost immediately, he grasped what was in her mind and said, 'I have a sitting-room upstairs.'

'Oh . . . I see.' She had known that very rich people did have sitting-rooms as well as bedrooms when they stayed at hotels. But their exclusive milieu was so unlike the world she inhabited that she hadn't automatically assumed that, even with a visitor, he would breakfast in private.

A suspicion of amusement glinted in his dark eyes as he added, 'You have no objection to breakfasting *à deux*, have you, Mrs Walker?'

Conscious of her provincialism, she flushed. 'Not at all.'

She had already noticed that his run in the park had left a glistening film of sweat on his face and neck. In the confined space of the lift, she could smell the forgotten aroma emanated by a clean, fit man after strenuous exertion. It was not unlike the sweet, earthy tang of cut grass. The last time she had stood near a man and been conscious of the heat and power of his body, and that strangely erotic male fragrance, had been after playing tennis with Chris.

It was only very rarely these days that some sight or sound would suddenly conjure the past. But now, as she stood in the lift, she remembered, as if it were yesterday, a hot summer afternoon when she and Chris and two friends had played a well-matched game on the hard court at his parents' farm.

They had been so young, so carefree. Never dreaming . . .

Swiftly she shut out the other, the nightmare memories, forcing herself to concentrate on the man she had come to see.

The black sweatband across his forehead, combined with his colouring and the angular structure of his face, brought to mind the American Indians with their bronzed skin and prominent cheekbones.

It wasn't until they had entered his spacious sitting-room, and he had picked up a telephone and was giving instructions about her breakfast, that she realised he didn't have an American accent.

'I'll be with you in ten minutes. Please make yourself at home,' he said, before he left her alone.

Looking round the làrge, luxurious room, she was struck by the restful atmosphere created by the use of neutral colours, mainly ivory and pale sand.

Impractical colours her mother would have called them. Mary Campbell liked patterned carpets which didn't show marks, and floral slip-covers and curtains. Fond as she was of her mother, Suzy didn't share her taste in furnishings, and this room appealed to her greatly.

Her mind boggled at what it must cost to stay in such accommodation. She could see that everything from the dense wool pile under her feet to the full, floor-length pale linen curtains was of the best possible quality. If the black and gold lacquer cabinet and the other antiques were reproductions, they would still have been very expensive. Everything about the room suggested a country house drawing-room rather than part of a hotel.

The most remarkable feature were the paintings; of which perhaps the most striking was a large and beautiful nude—a woman lying on a bed in a room where almost-closed shutters transmuted the bright light outside them into a subaqueous gloom in which her languid limbs glowed with the same soft lustre as the carvings on the giltwood mirror hanging on another wall.

This painting was not the only representation of the female body. There were two other pictures of naked women, and also a couple of sculptures, one in bronze and the other in stone. It seemed to her slightly odd to find five nudes in a hotel room, but perhaps it had been a whim of the designer commissioned to decorate the suite.

Having studied the pictures, Suzy turned her attention to the books, and again she found it surprising for a hotel to provide its patrons with such a catholic selection of reading matter.

She was looking through a book on Islamic art when she heard the sound of a key in the lock of the suite's outer door. A few moments later a waiter wheeled in a trolley.

On seeing her, he said, 'Good morning, madam.'

'Good morning.'

Suzy watched him remove an azalea in a porcelain cachepot from a semi-circular side table. He then moved the table into a space near the windows, lifted the flap which converted it into a round table, and covered the polished mahogany first with a thick felt pad and then with a white damask cloth.

Within minutes he had laid two places, plugged in an electric percolator, and moved two Regency armchairs from their places to either side of the table.

It was done without haste but with such efficiency that, as the clock began to chime the hour, he had only one thing left to do, and this was to remove a dark red carnation from a specimen vase, dry the stalk and place the flower on the table.

At the first stroke of eight o'clock, the inner door opened and Wolfe Vyner reappeared.

'Good morning, Barnes. How are you?'

'Can't complain, sir, thank you. How are you keeping, sir?'

'Very well, thanks.' He picked up the carnation and drew the stalk through the buttonhole of his coat.

He was wearing a dark grey suit with a pink shirt and grey tie. Having settled the flower in position, he came across the room to Suzy.

'Now we can shake hands, Mrs Walker.'

With his dark hair no longer dishevelled, his high, clever forehead exposed, and his athletic build made less noticeable by the formal, perfectly tailored clothes, he looked disconcertingly different. As his hand closed firmly over hers she was conscious that here was not merely a dynamic physical presence but a powerful intellectual force.

She felt that, if this man chose, his mind could pierce hers like a laser beam. The panel of senior executives who had tested her general knowledge and questioned her on her attitude to her work had not been as daunting as he was. She knew she had been over-confident in deciding to turn down his offer. Now it seemed to her much more likely that she wouldn't pass muster with him.

'What time do you normally get up in the morning, Mrs Walker?' he asked, as they moved to the table.

'In winter at seven. Usually earlier in the summer.'

He indicated where she should sit, and she flashed a smile at the waiter as he drew out her chair and, when she was ready, pushed it in for her.

'I always get up at six. If it's not light enough to go jogging, I work at my desk until it is.' As the waiter unfolded her napkin and draped it across her lap, Mr Vyner dealt with his own. 'I don't need a great deal of sleep. How about you?' he enquired.

'I have eight hours as a rule.'

She glanced at the large bowl of fruit—pieces of peach and orange mixed with cherries, green figs and glistening prunes—on to which he was spooning thick yogurt.

He said, 'After I'd seen you on TV, I read various newspaper reports which provided a fairly comprehensive curriculum vitae. But there are one or two gaps I'd like you to fill in for me.'

'Certainly, but I think I should point out first that I already have a job which I like and which is well paid. What made you think I might want to change it, Mr Vyner?'

'Perhaps you didn't—yesterday. But the post I think you might fill—and I emphasise might at this stage—is a much better one than you have at present. Unless you don't want to see the world, and to earn more than twice your present salary.'

'Do you know my present salary?' she asked, in surprise.

Yesterday, during the Press interview, she had been asked what she earned but had tactfully avoided a specific reply. She had also smilingly declined to pull up her skirt and cross her long, slender legs.

'No, but I can guess.' He suggested a figure which was very close to what she was paid.

'Yes ... about that,' she agreed, dipping a spoon into her grapefruit. 'Why is your present secretary leaving you, Mr Vyner?'

'Although she isn't a young woman, she's decided to marry,' he answered. 'I'd hoped to retain her services until she retired. However, at the age of forty, she's become involved with a widower with three teenage children. I think she may well regret giving up her freedom, but I can't persuade her to change her mind. How long is it since your husband died?'

'Three years.'

'The newspapers quote you as saying that you have no plans to remarry at the present time. Is that correct?'

'Yes, quite correct.'

He raised his dark eyes from his fruit and gave her an appraising look which seemed to include every detail from the small pearls she wore in her ears to the colourless varnish on her nails.

'Undoubtedly you will remarry, but perhaps not for several years. I should make it clear to you now that I don't pay an exceptionally high salary for the routine nine-to-five duties which occupy you at present. I work at least twice as hard as most people, and I expect my staff to do the same. There's no question of fixed hours, or fixed days off. The job would play havoc with your social life. But there would be certain compensating perquisites. You would live in the same hotels where I live. You would always travel first class; and several months of each year would be spent in the sun, in the Caribbean or the Pacific.'

Suzy decided to make no comment at this stage. In some ways the job sounded almost too good to be true. As far as she was concerned, long hours and erratic leisure were not major snags. But perhaps there were other disadvantages which hadn't come to light yet.

'Where is your home when you're not travelling, Mr Vyner?' she asked.

'In the conventional sense, I haven't one. In London, this is my home,' he said, with a gesture encompassing the elegant room. 'For me home is any place where I can live in comfort. I don't feel the common compulsion to own the roof over my head, although I do like to have a few personal possessions around me—paintings, books and so on.'

His use of the expression 'any place' rather than the English 'anywhere' prompted her to say, 'I was told that you operated on both sides of the Atlantic. I'm not clear which is your homeland.'

Having finished eating the fruit, he touched his napkin to his lips before leaning back in his chair. The gesture drew her attention to the shape of his wide, well-cut mouth.

'I think of myself as a citizen of the world, Mrs Walker. It's a pity everyone doesn't. Where we were born, or the country which issued our passport, has little bearing on the kind of people we are. When you fly, as I did yesterday, at an altitude from which you can see the curvature of the earth, and the sky outside the aeroplane blends into the blackness of space, it makes you realise that nationality is an archaic concept

of benefit only to politicians and other power-mongers
To misquote Rudyard Kipling—*Ours is the Earth and
everything that's in it*. There should be no frontiers; no
barriers between one place and another. We shouldn't
need to ask permission from the bureaucrats to go
where we please and live in the way we prefer.'

'But would that be practical?' she asked.

'Why not?'

Before she could translate her instinctive reaction
into a reasoned reply, the waiter reappeared with
several covered dishes on a tray.

It was obvious from their moist fluffy texture that
her scrambled eggs had been cooked only minutes
beforehand. Piled on buttered toast and garnished
with watercress, they looked delicious and made her
realise that her walk had made her very hungry.

Mr Vyner was having kippers for his breakfast—two
pairs of them, with side dishes of mushrooms and
grilled tomatoes. Clearly his appetite matched his tall,
broad-shouldered frame.

When they were alone again, instead of repeating his
question and forcing her to marshal her thoughts
rather than starting to eat, as she was eager to, he let
her off the hook by saying, 'Perhaps it's easier for me
to shed that divisive sense of nationality, because of
my eight great-grandparents only three came from the
same country. A couple of generations later that
mixture had been reduced to an American father and a
British mother, but the strains are still there in my
blood. What's your family background? Are both your
parents from Yorkshire?'

'No, my father is a Scot and my mother was born in
the West Country.'

'What does your father do for a living?'

'He's a veterinary surgeon—or was. He retired two
months ago.'

'That suggests you have older brothers and sisters.'

'Three sisters. The eldest one's husband was my father's partner and is now his successor. The other two are married to local farmers.'

'And you're employed by a firm which makes farm machinery. It sounds as if you're a close-knit family with a lot in common.'

'Yes, I suppose we are.'

'You've worked for the same company ever since you left school, I believe?'

'Yes.' She decided to be frank with him. 'At first I didn't see it as a career. It was merely a way of earning pin money until I married. At that stage my ambition was to be a wife and a mother. Later, after my husband's death, I had to have something to occupy me. I threw myself into the job to take my mind off ... what had happened. After a while I found I was actually enjoying it, and wanting to do it as well as possible. After a year in the general office, I was promoted to secretary to the works manager. I've been with him ever since.'

'Then it's high time you had a change,' Mr Vyner said briskly, as he opened the napkin enfolding the contents of a basket. Inside were crusty brown rolls. He offered them to her. 'I've no doubt you're extremely efficient—within the limits of your experience. But to justify your title of Britain's top secretary, you need to broaden your experience.'

'I know I do,' she agreed. 'But until recently I've been needed at home. My mother is quite badly disabled, and she can't run the house without help. Now that my father is at home all day the situation has changed. He's always been a domesticated man, but with a large veterinary practice to run, he didn't have the time or the energy to do all the things he does now.'

'So, apart from whatever notice you've contracted to give your employers, you are now at liberty to leave

Yorkshire whenever you choose?' he said, breaking a roll into pieces and helping himself to butter.

'Not entirely.'

He raised a dark eyebrow. 'Why not?'

'I've worked for my boss for a long time. I think it would be less than loyal to leave him at a month's notice, regardless of whether he could find a suitable replacement in that time. I'm sure your secretary isn't leaving you in the lurch, Mr Vyner.'

'No, she has to give me three months' notice. One of the reasons she's not travelling with me on this trip is because she has to weed out the applicants for her job. Sixty-four of them. By the time I return to New York, they'll have been reduced to half a dozen.'

'In that case, why bother with me?'

'Because I was favourably impressed by your behaviour on television. It's a medium which is very revealing of unattractive characteristics. You came over as a pleasant personality, not easily flustered and with a sense of humour. Combined with your professional qualifications, those are assets which make you an excellent candidate for the post. How good is your French?'

He asked this last question in French, to which she replied, in the same language, 'Not bad. Perhaps a little old-fashioned. I have an hour's conversation every week with an elderly Frenchwoman who lives near us. But she hasn't lived in France for years, and she isn't the sort of person who would use modern idioms anyway. Would working for you involve using my French?'

'Frequently. I shall be in Paris tomorrow and spend several days there. Your Spanish would be exercised, too, both in Spain and in Latin-America. Would you describe yourself as a gregarious person, Mrs Walker? Or do you prefer your own company?'

She suspected that these two questions were not as

straightforward as they sounded. She thought about them for some moments before she answered, 'I would rather be by myself than in uncongenial company, but given the choice between a good book and a party, I'd settle for the book.'

'Have you any portable hobbies other than reading? Hannah, my present secretary, has two—photography and needlework. She considers them essential resources in cities where she has no social contacts and where, at weekends, she may have a good deal of spare time while I'm visiting friends.'

'No, I haven't any hobbies at present. With studying for the Diploma, helping my mother run the house and babysitting for my sisters, I've had very little spare time. I imagine that—if you were to engage me, Mr Vyner—all the leisure time I might have could be spent, very enjoyably, in sightseeing. To begin to know London well would take several months of exploring.'

'Certainly: but there are times when it can be useful to amuse yourself without going out. There's always television, of course.' His shrug and the twist of his lips expressed his opinion of that pastime.

Having finished her scrambled eggs, Suzy found her hunger satisfied. She accepted a second cup of coffee, but declined to try the dark, thick-cut marmalade or the black cherry jam.

Mr Vyner sampled both, leaving only one roll in the basket.

'Do you smoke, Mrs Walker?' he enquired.

'No, I don't.'

'Very sensible. Neither do I, and I see no reason to tolerate the habit in others.'

'Would you mind if I asked you some questions?'

'You've already asked one,' he reminded her. 'Go ahead, ask what you please.'

'I know you're a leading financier, but I'm afraid I

don't know what kind of financier. What are your particular interests?'

'Anything profitable,' he answered. 'My interests vary from country to country and almost from year to year. In the times we live in, it's necessary to be extremely flexible . . . and not to have all one's eggs in the same basket. To give you some random examples, the companies under my aegis include a Belgian chocolate factory, a couple of health farms in England, a racing and breeding stud in Virginia and a motor yacht yard in Italy.' He smiled at her. 'If you want to check me out, you won't find it difficult.'

He put a hand inside his coat and produced a slim black leather wallet and a black pen. From the wallet he extracted a card, on the back of which he wrote a name and number.

'This number will put you through to the secretary to the Governor of the Bank of England. It was she who contacted the man who contacted you last night. She'll vouch for my bona fides.'

As he passed the card across the table, Suzy said, 'I didn't mean to suggest that——'

'You're very wise to be cautious,' he interrupted. 'Both in Europe and in America there are businessmen whose outward probity screens both highly disreputable and, in some cases, criminal activities.' He offered her the pen and another card. 'Would you write down your home address and telephone number.'

As she did so the inner door opened. She looked up to see a tall, beautiful, auburn-haired woman in a man's silk dressing gown strolling into the room. At the sight of Suzy she stopped short, looking faintly perplexed.

Wolfe Vyner rose to his feet. 'Good morning. You're up very early.' He crossed the room to where she stood and bent to kiss her on the cheek. With his arm round her waist, he turned to introduce Suzy.

'This is Mrs Walker whom you may have seen in the newspapers yesterday. She's won a gold medal for her secretarial skills. I asked her to breakfast to discuss the possibility of her replacing Hannah. I did mention it to you last night.'

'Oh, yes, so you did. I forgot.' The woman leaned lightly against him, her cloud of hair brushing his shoulder. 'How do you do, Mrs Walker. Congratulations on the gold medal.'

'How do you do. Thank you, Mrs Vyner,' said Suzy.

As she finished writing her address, she heard him say to his wife, 'I have to leave in five minutes. I can meet you for lunch. Where would you like to have it?'

'I'll be shopping in Knightsbridge this morning. The Berkeley would suit me.'

'The Berkeley at one. Shall I order your breakfast?'

'No, I haven't had my bath yet. I'll have breakfast later. I don't know what woke me up. *Must* you go out so early, darling?'

She spoke in a soft, purring tone which made Suzy think she wanted to take him back to bed with her.

'I'm afraid so. I have an appointment in the City at nine-thirty. We can spend the afternoon together.'

Without looking up, Suzy knew they were exchanging messages with their eyes. Leaving the card on the table, she rose and, without glancing in their direction, went to retrieve her bag and cardigan.

When, ready to leave, she did look at them, he and his wife had moved apart.

'Thank you for breakfast, Mr Vyner,' she said politely.

He said, 'Where are you going next? Perhaps I can give you a lift.'

'Thank you, but I'm going to the Tower of London to see the Crown Jewels. I can get there by the Underground.'

'The London Underground in the rush hour is almost as hellish as the Subway in New York. The only civilised underground train system that I know—fortunately it's not a method of transport I've had to use much—is the Subway in Toronto. The Tower's not far out of my way. I'll drop you off,' he said firmly.

Turning to his wife, he added, 'Mrs Walker may want to wash her hands. Show her the bathroom, would you, Belinda. I have to get my briefcase.'

Belinda, obviously naked under the dark green silk robe, led the way to a lavatory off the lobby.

As she retouched her lipstick, Suzy wondered if Mr Vyner was always considerate of other people's possible needs, or if he had wanted a few minutes in which to give Belinda a swift foretaste of the pleasures in store for her later.

She wondered how long they had been married. Not long, judging by the vibrations between them. She could never remember being as keenly aware of two people's desire for each other.

Her sisters had not been married many years, and sometimes, when she had been babysitting for them, they would come home relaxed and happy after an evening of freedom from domestic concerns. But she could not remember them or their husbands exuding the sensual promise which had been in the air a few minutes ago.

As she turned back the cuffs of her shirt and lathered her hands with a new cake of Culpeper's lemon verbena soap, she felt certain that, in their bedroom, the Vyners were embracing.

To her surprise and discomfiture, her imagination presented her with a clear, detailed picture of the silk robe lying on the floor while Belinda shivered voluptuously as her husband's brown hands caressed her, and their mouths fused in a long kiss.

It was like seeing a love scene on television or at the cinema. It made Suzy achingly conscious of her own uncaressed, unloved body. Sometimes, not very often, her need for physical affection was almost a pain.

Now, with thirty only six years ahead, she felt she might never meet someone to assuage her longing for fulfilment. She had missed the boat, as the saying went. It seemed the best she could hope for was to be someone's second wife, and perhaps, like Hannah, a stepmother.

Belinda Vyner did not reappear to say goodbye. Going down in the lift, Suzy wondered if she was his first wife, and if she minded always living in hotels. Presumably they had no children, unless he had some by a previous marriage.

A black Rolls-Royce was waiting for them. The driver saluted. 'Good morning, sir.'

' 'Morning, Rivers. I want to drop Mrs Walker at the Tower before we go to Lombard Street.'

'Very good, sir.'

'Are you particularly interested in jewels?' Wolfe Vyner asked her, as the limousine glided away from the steps outside the hotel.

'I wouldn't say that, but the Crown Jewels are rather special and the Tower is so steeped in history that it seems something not to be missed. Have you been there?'

'No, that period of English history doesn't interest me. If I have an hour or two to spare, I prefer to spend it in the art galleries.'

He crossed his long legs and she noticed his gleaming black loafers and the elegance of his ankles in grey silk socks.

The traffic now was much heavier than it had been when she had walked through Mayfair. However, once they reached what she knew must be the Embankment running alongside the Thames, the Rolls-Royce was

able to speed up, although it moved so smoothly and
quietly that, had there been no other vehicles on the
road, she would not have realised how fast they were
travelling.

'Which of the galleries do you consider the best?'
she asked.

'Are you asking about those which sell paintings,
or the art museums?'

'The art museums.'

For the rest of the way to the Tower he discussed
the comparative merits of London's many fine art
collections. It was clear that he was a connoisseur.
Once again Suzy was conscious of her own lack of
sophistication.

As he had made no further reference to the reason
for their meeting, she concluded he considered her
unsuitable.

She was surprised when he said, 'Am I to take it
from what you said during breakfast that, at the
present time, you aren't interested in changing your
job, Mrs Walker?'

Suddenly she knew that she did want the job as
his secretary. She wanted it very much.

'Oh, no—I didn't mean that at all,' she said hastily.
'In fact as Mr Howard, whom I work for now, is
retiring before long, I *am* thinking about a change. But
I couldn't leave before he does.'

'I see.' He leaned forward to speak to his driver. 'No
need for you to get out, Rivers. You can keep the
engine running. I'll only be a minute or two.'

This was as the car drew up near the entrance to the
Tower. As soon as it stopped, he sprang out and
waited for her to follow him.

'The Tower may not open until ten,' he said, as she
alighted.

'It opens at half past nine. I don't mind waiting.
Thank you for the lift, Mr Vyner.'

'My pleasure.' Instead of shaking hands and saying goodbye, he walked away from the car. 'I'll add your name to the short list and let you know my decision as soon as possible,' he told her.

Suzy hoped her face didn't reveal the excitement and hope which flared inside her.

'Thank you,' she said evenly.

He did shake hands with her then; looking down at her with that curiously penetrating scrutiny which she found it hard to meet with composure.

'Goodbye, Mrs Walker.' His suntanned hand gripped hers firmly but did not crush it.

She smiled. 'Goodbye.'

'By the way, I'm not married,' he said, before he released her fingers and turned away.

CHAPTER TWO

'So? How did your day go? Are you exhausted?' asked Alix, when they met for a pre-theatre supper at another inexpensive restaurant.

Suzy said, 'I was before I had a bath. My goodness, the Underground in the rush hour *is* hellish! I've never been so squashed and jostled in my life, and being laden with shopping didn't help.' She remembered it wasn't her friend who had told her that. 'However, I did start the day being driven around in a Rolls,' she added.

Alix lifted her eyebrows. 'How come?'

Suzy explained, beginning with the message waiting for her the night before.

'My God! That's marvellous, Suzy. What did I tell you? I said something like this might happen, and it has. I wonder how long he'll keep you in suspense?'

'I don't know, but I do know one thing. If I told Dad and Mother everything which happened during the interview, they'd have a fit and want me to turn the job down.'

'What do you mean?' asked Alix, intrigued.

Suzy told her about the woman she had mistaken for Wolfe Vyner's wife.

'Who do you think she was? A high-class call-girl or his regular girl-friend?'

'Oh, his regular girl-friend, obviously. He's not the kind of man who would ever have to pay for sex.'

'You mean he's attractive?'

'Very.'

'Wow! An attractive, unmarried, rich financier. There has to be a catch.'

'I should imagine the catch is that he's totally selfish.'

'Who wouldn't be, if they could? If I could live life *my* way, down to the very last detail, I would—and so would most people. You're not going to tell your parents about her, are you?'

'No. If I do get the job—and I probably shan't—I don't want them worrying about my working for someone they'd think immoral. I saw her again later on.'

'Really? Where?'

'In Harrods. I went there after the Tower. Just as I was going in, she was coming out. She looked right through me. It was rather deflating not to be recognised so soon after meeting her.'

'How did she look with her clothes on?'

'Fabulous. She was wearing a stunning coat-dress of very soft pale grey suede, and her shoes and bag ... everything about her was perfection. She smelt marvellous, too. As I passed her, there was a lovely gust of scent. But I didn't much like the way she swept through the swing doors without looking behind her to see if anyone else was coming,' Suzy added thoughtfully.

'No, I can't stand people who do that,' Alix agreed. 'Or who, when you hold a door for them, stalk past without saying thank you. How old is he?'

'I'm not sure. Around thirty-five, but terrifically fit. Not a candidate for a coronary. He ate an enormous breakfast, but none of it was junk food. I should think he takes pretty good care of himself.'

An hour later, as they sat in the circle of a Shaftesbury Avenue theatre, waiting for the curtain to go up on a play acclaimed by the critics as the wittiest comedy London had seen for many seasons, Suzy suddenly clutched her friend's arm.

'There they are!'

'Who?'

'Mr Vyner and Belinda. Just arriving at the right-hand side of the second row.'

At that moment the house lights dimmed. The tall, good-looking couple making their way towards two empty seats in the second row of the stalls could only be seen in silhouette.

It was not until the first interval, when they left their seats to merge with the slow-moving throng heading for the bar, that Alix was able to see them for long enough to say, 'Her face seems familiar. I'm sure I've seen her before. I see what you mean about her clothes—get a load of that little number!'

Suzy murmured agreement. Tonight Belinda was wearing a clinging dress of black chiffon. The sleeves and the top half of the bodice were unlined, showing the upper curves of her breasts and the valley between them through the filmy silk chiffon. Round her neck she wore a skein of freshwater pearls with the jewelled clasp at the front, and diamond ear-rings winked as she turned her head to smile up at the man close behind her.

'He's tanned, but she's not, which suggests that she's not his constant companion,' said Alix, as they made their way to the circle bar where two glasses of red wine, ordered earlier, were waiting for them. 'You say she was wearing his dressing gown. *That* suggests that she hadn't been expecting to spend the night with him. Perhaps their affair is just starting. They may have met at a party. He suggested a nightcap at his place, and they ended up spending the night together.'

Suzy shook her head. 'I don't think so. In that case I shouldn't have taken her for his wife. There was something about his attitude, and hers, which gave me the impression they had a . . . a definite relationship. Neither of them was the slightest bit embarrassed by her strolling in with me there.'

Alix grinned. 'This is London, not Brockthorpe, Suzy. There are people in this city who wouldn't be embarrassed if you caught them in the middle of an orgy. They'd just say, "Hi! Care to join us?" You'll have to stop being naïve when you start to mingle with the jet set.'

'Do I seem very naïve to you?'

'You do rather—yes,' Alix told her, with friendly candour. 'How can you not be?—living at home as you do. Your parents are dears, but they are a bit stuffy, you know. So are Rosalie and Helen and Judith. I sometimes wonder if any of them realise there is a world beyond Brockthorpe, and that husbands and babies are not the only options for women now.'

It seemed to Suzy that for Alix to be critical of her sisters for the conventional domesticity of their lives was a rather glaring piece of double-think when, if only Mike were willing, she would instantly give up her nursing career to become a wife and mother.

But she kept this reflection to herself, saying only, 'If people live in a peaceful backwater like Brockthorpe, it's dangerously easy to follow the accepted patterns and become resistant to changes. Something Mr Vyner said to me this morning made me realise how seldom I question the way things are, or think about whether they might be better another way. He made me feel very woolly-minded. And when he was talking about art on the way to the Tower, I felt horribly ignorant.'

'Why was he talking about art?'

'It's one of his interests.' She told Alix about the five nudes in his sitting-room at the Connaught.

During the second interval, Wolfe Vyner and his companion remained in their places, as did she and Alix. She found it difficult to take her eyes off them.

It was Belinda who did most of the talking. Her thick auburn hair which, when Suzy had seen her in

Knightsbridge, had been loose on her shoulders, now
was pinned up in an arrangement too elaborate to be
her own handiwork. It had to have been done by a top
stylist. Compared with the hair of the other women in
the stalls, hers was strikingly lustrous and alive, as was
the dark, almost black hair of the man listening to her.

Even seen from behind they stood out from the rest
of the audience. Suzy had heard the term 'the
beautiful people' applied to the rich and privileged,
but this was the first time she had seen, in the flesh,
anyone who exemplified the expression.

Like cosseted pedigree dogs they both had an air of
being in superb condition. As Belinda illustrated her
remarks with expressive movements of her hands,
Suzy could see that she wore several dramatic-looking
rings, and her long nails were the colour of garnets.

In Suzy's experience only women who never had to
do any housework had nails like that. She guessed that
Belinda's hands were silky-soft and fragrant with
expensive hand lotion.

Just as she was thinking this, she saw Wolfe Vyner
capture one of Belinda's hands and carry it to his lips
in a manner which suggested that, even if she was his
mistress and never likely to be anything else, he felt a
certain tenderness towards her.

By the following evening Suzy was back with her
family. At first her parents and her sisters and
brothers-in-law—who had been invited to supper—
seemed eager to hear about her trip. But even before
the meal was over their interest was waning and the
conversation was turning to what had happened in her
absence. After the meal they all settled down to watch
the latest instalment of a long-running television saga.

'It's nice to have you back with us, dear,' Mrs
Campbell said comfortably, as her youngest daughter
settled herself on a cushion on the floor beside her

mother's chair. 'I know you're a sensible girl, and not likely to run any risks, but one hears of such nasty things happening in big cities nowadays. Muggings and so on.'

Suzy watched the screen with the others, but her thoughts were elsewhere. She realised that although they were quite proud of her achievement, and glad she had had a good time, and pleased with the presents she had brought them, fundamentally they all shared her mother's relief that she had returned and life could continue as before.

One aspect of the trip she hadn't mentioned was her interview with Wolfe Vyner. She had made up her mind in the train not to say anything to them until she heard from him. Probably, when he returned to New York, Hannah would have drawn up a short list of candidates with far more impressive qualifications than her own.

Meanwhile there was little point in kindling their resistance to a change which might never come about. Although, even if she received a 'regret to inform you the vacancy has been filled' letter from him, she had come home determined to take his advice and broaden her experience.

Her family weren't going to like it when she told them she was leaving Brockthorpe, but she knew it was something she had to do. She had lingered too long already; the longer she delayed, the harder it would be to break free. Winning the gold medal had forced her out of the rut, but it would be all too easy to sink back into it.

A few days after her return, Suzy received a brief note from Alix. Enclosed with it was a page torn from a glossy magazine.

At first Suzy couldn't make out why her friend should have sent her a description of a society wedding. She turned the page over. On this side were half a dozen pictures of people at a country house dance. One of them Alix had ringed.

The caption read *Colonel Sir John Fox and Lady Belinda Stratton, sister of the Earl of Ormskirk.*

Even when bored, Belinda looked strikingly beautiful. The photograph was in colour. She was wearing a blouse of white organdie with huge sleeves, a full black taffeta skirt and a wide sash of crimson silk. Long diamond ear-rings accentuated the sweep of her long white neck.

Alix had scrawled—*Thought this would interest you. Any word from your tycoon yet? I'm keeping my fingers crossed for you.*

'Who's your letter from, dear?' asked her mother.

The postman came to the Campbell's house while they were having breakfast, and after they had heard the rattle of the letter-box it was always Mr Campbell who fetched the post from the doormat inside the front door. Most of the mail was for him, with occasional letters to his wife from her relations.

It was impossible for Suzy to receive a letter without her parents knowing about it; and although she knew her mother's question was prompted by affectionate interest, nevertheless it vexed her a little that, at twenty-four, she had no privacy.

Because of Mrs Campbell's difficulty in walking, the telephone was in the sitting-room where she spent most of her time. Which meant that Suzy could never receive a call without one or both her parents listening in to her side of the conversation. Not that it mattered, because few people ever telephoned her, and never about anything which she didn't want her parents to know.

But it was the principle which had begun, suddenly, to irk her.

'It's only a note from Alix.' She could see that her

mother was curious about the tear-out from the magazine. It was impossible to explain the real reason why she had sent it. She handed it across the table, saying with a twinge of guilt at the fabrication, 'She's thinking of copying that outfit.'

Mrs Campbell studied the picture. 'I like what she's wearing, but I don't like her sulky expression. Is Alix going to a big dance?'

'Er ... the hospital ball, I expect.' Suzy pushed back her chair. 'I must be off.'

That evening, with a magnifying glass belonging to her father, she studied Lady Belinda's face in close-up. She felt her mother was mistaken in describing her expression as sulky. Nor was she bored, as Suzy herself had first thought. Studied more closely, she looked unhappy.

Perhaps she was in the same situation as Alix—in love with a man who didn't want to commit himself to any one woman.

It was all very well for feminist propagandists to exhort women not to tie themselves down to marriage and motherhood without considering all the other possibilities open to them. The snag about that was that falling in love wasn't an option. It wasn't something one chose to do. It happened, like an accident, or being infected by a virus.

Alix couldn't stop herself loving Mike, and it might be that Belinda Stratton had lost her heart to Wolfe Vyner and couldn't retrieve it.

Suzy wondered if her family knew about the liaison, and if they disapproved. She had put the other woman's age in the very late twenties. She might even be thirty. What had prevented her marrying when she was younger? The daughters of the aristocracy usually married in their early twenties, especially the beauties. As the days passed, and no letter came from New

York, Suzy's hopes dwindled.

She began to buy *The Times* on her way to work. At night, in her bedroom, she studied the columns headed *La Crème de la crème* in which the top jobs for secretaries and personal assistants were advertised.

ENG/SPANISH P.A./SEC. Knightsbridge— £9,000. Busy demanding position as PA/Sec to vice-president of newly established London office of an American Oil Co. S/hand Eng. essential. Age 25-35.

That sounded a possibility. She made a note of the staff consultants who were advertising the job, and their telephone number.

PERSONAL ASSISTANT to 2 American lawyers in period Mayfair building. Top secretarial skills, mature outlook, initiative and administrative ability are required. Bookkeeping & experience on memory typewriter would be a distinct advantage. £7,500 plus medical insurance, luncheon vouchers and 4 weeks holiday.

TOP SECRETARY required to handle London office of International Group chairman. Marble Arch area. Must have experience of bookkeeping, international money movement, typing, shorthand and telex. Capable of working with full autonomy. Top salary negotiable.

The other advertisements which she studied were those in the *Rentals* column. These made it clear that although the salaries offered sounded high, so were the rents of London flats. Either she would have to share, or live beyond walking distance of where she worked.

When ten days had gone by, she came to the disturbing conclusion that Mr Vyner was not even going to notify her that the job had been given to someone else. She could hardly believe that a man of his standing in the world would behave with such lack of courtesy and, although she had given up hope of getting the job now, she continued to put off applying for any of the posts she had seen advertised.

One evening, soon after she had arrived home, she was in her room changing her suit for a sweater and jeans, when her father called up the staircase, 'Telephone, Suzy!'

She expected it to be a call from one of her sisters. Sometimes, when they and their husbands made spur-of-the-moment decisions to go out for the evening, they would ring up just about now to ask her to babysit.

When she entered the sitting-room, her mother was holding the receiver. With her hand covering the mouthpiece, and a puzzled expression on her face, Mrs Campbell said, 'It's a call from Paris for you. A Mr Vyner.'

CHAPTER THREE

As she sat in the special departure lounge reserved for passengers on Concorde, Suzy wondered if anyone else there had arrived at Heathrow by Underground train.

Watching her fellow travellers—most of them men—removing their overcoats and relaxing with dry Martinis or whatever else they chose to order, she thought it unlikely. Those who had not been driven to the airport in their own or their company's cars had undoubtedly arrived by taxi.

However, as her train from Yorkshire had arrived in London at two o'clock and the flight to New York didn't take off until six, there had been plenty of time for her to come to Heathrow by the least expensive means of transport.

Although she was about to become the highly-paid secretary of one of the world's richest men, she had no intention of wasting money. Moreover, she was not yet on contract. That would come later, after she had proved her worth during a three months' probationary period.

As she drank the coffee brought to her by the ground stewardess who had taken away her raincoat, she wondered what time Wolfe Vyner would arrive.

He was coming over from Paris on a flight which would land just in time for him to board Concorde. Knowing Air France also had a supersonic service to America by which he could have travelled direct, she was forced to conclude that he was putting himself out for her benefit.

The prospect of meeting him again sent a tremor of

nervous excitement through her. She still found it hard to believe he had chosen her from all the other applicants.

For the umpteenth time since the evening he had telephoned to tell her the job was hers, she wondered if she would prove equal to it. It wasn't that she lacked confidence in her abilities, but rather that she suspected Mr Vyner of being an exceptionally exacting man who drove himself to the limit and expected a similar performance from all his subordinates.

Twenty-five minutes before take-off, the passengers started boarding. Suzy wondered what she should do if, for some reason, her employer failed to arrive in time. It could be that his flight from France had been delayed. But in that case, surely he would have telephoned?

'Are you ready to board, Mrs Walker?' the stewardess asked, coming across the lounge and picking up the empty coffee cup.

'I'm waiting for my employer.'

'Yes, but Mr Vyner sometimes cuts it rather fine. I should go aboard now if I were you,' said the girl, with a friendly smile.

'Good evening, Mrs Walker. This way, please.' An equally friendly cabin stewardess showed her to her seat.

In the aircraft there were only two seats on either side of the aisle, and they had considerably more leg room than the package holiday aeroplanes on which Suzy had flown before.

She sat in the aisle seat, leaving the one by the window for Wolfe Vyner when he arrived. She glanced at her watch. Only ten minutes to go. At least, if he didn't turn up, she knew where to go at the other end.

His headquarters in New York was a suite at the Pierre Hotel. There she would find Miss Eisenhart, who hadn't retired yet. She was going to help Suzy settle in before she departed for Boston where her widower and his three children lived.

'Did you think I wasn't going to make it?'

She looked up to see Mr Vyner smiling down at her.

'Oh ... good evening. Yes, I was beginning to wonder if you might not.' She stood up, intending to move into the aisle while he took his place by the window.

'No, no—you have the porthole. I've seen the view many times.' He made an authoritative gesture for her to take the inside seat.

As they sat down and fastened their seatbelts, he said, 'I usually drink sherry before dinner, but as this is your first transatlantic flight, and the end of a tough week for me, I think we should celebrate.'

To her amazement, Suzy found herself taking off with a glass of champagne in her hand.

Unlike most of the passengers in their navy or grey bespoke suits, Mr Vyner had already exchanged the formal clothes of the boardroom for a cashmere sweater and pale beige cavalry twill pants. Not for the first time she was struck by his immaculately polished shoes; brown tassel loafers with the colour and sheen of a chestnut fresh from its husk.

She was glad she had remembered to run a tissue over her own slightly travel-dusty black pumps while tidying herself at the airport.

It took him only a few moments to decide what he was going to eat. But for Suzy, the gourmet menu, each course with several choices, called for longer consideration. She had scarcely made up her mind when he pointed out that the Machmeter was showing that, after barely twenty minutes in the air, they were travelling at almost six hundred and seventy mph or Mach One, the speed of sound.

'On the first supersonic flights, people used to start

cheering at this point,' he told her. 'Now the novelty
has worn off.'

'When did Concorde start flying? I can't remember.'

'In 1976.'

'Were you on the first flight?'

'Yes. As far as possible, I never fly any other way
now. Not only to avoid jet-lag. As I often work during
the night and take cat naps by day, ordinary flying
doesn't upset my circadian rhythms as much as it does
for people with conventional sleep patterns. It's the
eight hours of physical inactivity on an ordinary flight
which I dislike.'

After one of the four stewardesses had taken their
orders, he went on, 'As you probably realise, by New
York time we shall land an hour and a half before we
took off. Your rhythm won't be disturbed, except by
having your dinner several hours earlier than usual.'

Perhaps it was the champagne which prompted her
to reply, 'My sleep pattern is already upset. I hardly
slept a wink last night. I was too excited.'

Immediately, she regretted the childish confession.
Her naïveté was showing again, as unseemly in her
new position as the uneven hem of a slip. She must
learn not to make such admissions.

'Your family will miss you—and you them, no
doubt,' he remarked.

'Perhaps . . . a little. But it's time I branched out on
my own. I'm looking forward to it. Not for me, thank
you'—this as one of the stewardesses would have
refilled her glass.

'My parents divorced when I was three, remarried
and had other children. I have two families,' he told
her. 'As a child, I shuttled between them.'

Being given some personal details of his life made
her feel a little less foolish about her impulsive
confession. Yet, within a few seconds of telling herself

to think before she spoke, she made another unguarded remark.

'It must be very uncommon for anyone to be educated at an American prep school, an English public school and an American university,' she said.

Wolfe Vyner turned his dark head and gave her an amused glance. 'So you did check me out?'

'Only in *Who's Who*.'

The entry about him was clearly imprinted on her memory. He was thirty-seven. Birthplace, New York City. His father's name, Bradley Vyner, might be well known in America, but it hadn't meant anything to her. His mother had been the daughter of an English baronet and he, when she had looked him up in an earlier edition of *Who's Who*, had been married to a Frenchwoman.

Again, the name of Mr Vyner's first school had meant nothing to her. She had assumed it must be a leading preparatory school because later he had gone to Eton and, later still, to Harvard.

Clearly his achievements in the world of high finance had been made from the springboard of an affluent Establishment upbringing. At the same time there must be in him the same dynamic energy and driving force which activated men who, from humble origins, stormed their way to the summits of achievement.

'Perhaps it's a little unusual, but I'm sure it was a valuable experience to grow up with an intimate knowledge of two countries rather than one,' was his response to her statement. 'I also spent a lot of time in France with my grandmother. She's a Parisienne by birth, and she went back after my grandfather died. Now she's very old—in her eighties—but still a fascinating woman. You'll meet her next time we're there.'

Throughout the excellent meal—very different from

the plastic food served on most flights—he talked to her in a manner which was as friendly and easy as if they were equals rather than employer and employee.

By now they had reached Mach Two and were moving faster than a rifle bullet; although this was hard to believe in the seemingly motionless cabin. Suzy peered out of the porthole, gazing in wonder at the curve of the earth. She could almost believe they were travelling to another planet.

After dinner, Mr Vyner produced a book. He must have bought it in Paris. It was a biography of a Frenchman whose name was unknown to her. She made a mental note to look him up at the first opportunity.

There was no in-flight movie on Concorde, but there was a choice of five radio channels. Suzy moved her seat into the reclining position and settled back to listen to music.

'Time to wake up, Mrs Walker.'

As the deep male voice called her back from the dark outer space of unconsciousness, it also conjured a memory which her conscious mind had suppressed.

Halfway between sleeping and waking, she thought she was in the hospital, about to begin the long and terrible ordeal which had followed the accident.

She hadn't known then how much anguish she would have to bear, but this time she did. It was all there, stored in her memory—put away, but never forgotten. As the past of three years ago became confused with the present, she moaned and tried to slip back into the nothingness of sleep.

The voice wouldn't let her escape. 'Come on, Mrs Walker ... wake up!' A hand grasped her arm and shook it, not ungently but firmly enough to force her to open her eyes.

For a moment or two she blinked without

recognition at the face looking down into hers. This
was not the young doctor she remembered, nor was
she lying in a bed surrounded by screens. Could it be
she was still in the ambulance?

'Where are we?' she muttered, confused.

'In a few minutes' time we're going to be landing at
Kennedy. I thought you'd prefer to be woken before
we touch down. The noise made by reverse thrust can
be alarming if you're still half asleep.'

Her mind slipped back into gear. She knew where
she was and with whom. As Wolfe Vyner turned to
face forward, she sat up, realising that the champagne
before dinner and the wine with it had conspired to
help her catch up some of the sleep she had lost the
night before.

He had removed the headset she had been wearing
when she dozed off. She must have been sleeping very
heavily not to feel him do it. Had her mouth dropped
open? she wondered uneasily. Sleeping in a semi-
upright position was not a posture that flattered
people. It could make them look half-witted.

She hoped it had not given her the vacant
expression she had seen on other people's faces when
they napped in public. To go to sleep at all could not
be a point in her favour. Even though he had said that
sometimes he took a catnap, she felt sure he would not
have expected her to doze. Not a good start, she
thought vexedly, clenching her teeth against a yawn.

Not for Concorde passengers the queues and delays
often suffered by less pampered air travellers. In no
time at all Suzy's new black suitcase and matching
softbag had been restored to her. To her surprise, Mr
Vyner had had no baggage in the aircraft's hold.

'I don't need any when I'm travelling between
places where I have *pieds-à-terre*,' he explained.

She had expected to leave the airport in a large

limousine like the one he owned or hired in London. However, the last lap of the journey was by helicopter; a twenty-minute flight which avoided delays caused by traffic jams.

Most of the flight was over the borough of Queens, a sprawling suburb bordered by the East River. As the chopper crossed the river, heading for the East Side heliport, Suzy had her first close-up view of New York's famous skyline, still dominated, in midtown Manhattan, by the soaring pinnacle of the Empire State Building.

From the heliport to the Pierre Hotel on the east side of Central Park was a few minutes' ride in a cab.

As they entered the lobby a tall, dark-haired, elegant woman rose from a chair and came towards them.

Mr Vyner said, 'Hello, Hannah. This is Mrs Walker. I'll leave her in your hands now. I'll see you tomorrow, Mrs Walker.'

He walked away, leaving them together.

'I'm delighted to meet you, Mrs Walker,' said Miss Eisenhart, shaking hands. 'If you left your home twelve hours ago, you must be longing for a shower. It's the best way I know to recover from a long journey, although Mr Vyner wouldn't agree with me on that. He prefers to have a half-hour work-out before he gets under the shower.'

'I gathered he was keen on exercise. The first time I met him, he'd been jogging in Hyde Park,' said Suzy.

'Yes, he jogs every morning, wherever he is. Except when there's snow. Then he has to make do with an indoor work-out. And I guess he's right when he says that exercise generates vitality. As you'll start to find out tomorrow, he has incredible energy, both mental and physical. When everyone else is exhausted, Mr Vyner is still full of pep. The bell-boy will bring your bags up in the service elevator'—this as she ushered Suzy into one of the lifts.

The warmth and friendliness of her manner quickly put Suzy at ease. She had an immediate sense that Miss Eisenhart was an ally who would help her through the initial difficulties of adjusting to an unfamiliar environment.

It seemed that the usual registration procedure did not apply to a member of Mr Vyner's entourage. His secretary already held the key to Suzy's room. This, when they reached it, was not, as she had anticipated, one of the hotel's least well-situated bedrooms. To her pleased surprise, the window looked out on the treetops of the Park.

'The street below is Fifth Avenue, which is the dividing line between the East Side and the West Side,' Miss Eisenhart told her. 'The layout of Manhattan is very simple. You'll soon get to know your way around. Ah, here are your bags'—as a knock on the door was followed by the rattle of a pass-key.

When the bell-boy had transferred her baggage from his trolley to the luggage racks, Suzy gave him the tip she had had ready in her pocket.

'Why don't I start hanging your things up while you go take a shower?' suggested Miss Eisenhart. 'Then we'll both relax with a cocktail—or coffee, if you prefer it—and start getting acquainted.'

'That sounds lovely, and I would rather have coffee, if I may? I had champagne and wine on the plane, and I don't normally drink very much,' Suzy answered.

She unstrapped and unlocked her suitcase and took out the cotton caftan she used as a robe and which was the last thing she'd packed. Her toilet bag was packed in the centre of the softbag. Leaving Miss Eisenhart speaking to Room Service, she went into the lobby and opened the other door leading from it.

Her parents' house had only one bathroom which didn't have an overhead shower, merely a hand-spray which Suzy herself had had installed to facilitate washing her hair.

To have a bathroom for her exclusive use was a luxury; especially a bathroom such as this one where the thick towels were warm from hanging on a heated rail, and even a facecloth, shower cap and phials of shampoo and bath essence were provided.

By the time she returned to the bedroom, with her suit and blouse over her arm, Miss Eisenhart had almost completed unpacking for her. Even the folding leather frame with, on one side, a photograph of her parents and, on the other, of her husband, had been placed on the night table.

'It's very good of you to unpack for me. As you've seen, I haven't brought many clothes with me. I thought I might have to change my style of dressing to some extent, and that whatever I needed I could buy in New York,' Suzy told her.

Coming up in the lift she had noticed that the other woman was wearing a dark green silk shirt with a skirt of pleated wool crêpe in the identical colour. A single strand of large pearls with matching ear-studs, a simple but expensive-looking watch and a diamond ring on her engagement finger were her only pieces of jewellery. She had thin legs and narrow feet shod in plain dark green low-heeled pumps. High heels would have made her nearly as tall as Mr Vyner. In fact, although she gave an impression of elegance and charm, she was basically a too-tall, too-thin woman, and also a rather plain one who, as a girl, had probably despaired of her looks but had since come successfully to terms with them.

'Yes, New York is a great place to shop—if you know how to go about it. Not right now but some other time I'll let you into some secrets,' Miss Eisenhart promised. 'Judging by the things you've brought with you, you have very good taste. The one change you may want to make is to increase your fashion budget to include more designer clothes. When I was in my first job I had some excellent advice from another girl who now, twenty years later, is president of her own company. She said: 'Hannah, forget about fashion. Go for quality and classic styling. If you want to get to the top, you have to begin by dressing like a top person.' Which, somehow, Eileen managed to do—even when neither of us was earning much.'

Another knock at the outer door heralded the arrival of the coffee she had ordered.

'How long have you worked for Mr Vyner?' Suzy asked, when they were alone again.

'Twelve years. In some ways I'm sad to be leaving. He's an extraordinary man and there's never been a dull moment. But I didn't set out to have a career like the friend I just mentioned. My idea was to work for some years and then marry, have several children and maybe return to work when my family didn't need my full attention. However'—she shrugged her shoulders—'it didn't work out that way. But better late than never, I guess. As Mr Vyner may have told you, I'm about to be married to a dear man who lost his first wife, and who has three delightful children. Fortunately they don't seem to resent their father marrying again.'

The bedside telephone rang.

'That's probably for me,' said Miss Eisenhart, rising to answer it. After giving the room number and her name, she listened for several moments before saying, 'Yes, Mrs Sawyer, he's back. If the switchboard can't get him for you, it may be that he's taking a shower. I'm on another floor with Mr Vyner's new secretary who has just arrived from England. If you want to speak to him urgently, I can go up to the suite and ask him to call you back. No, it's no trouble at all. I'll go up right away.'

Replacing the receiver, she said to Suzy, 'You'll have to excuse me, Mrs Walker. Oh, look, shall we stop being formal and use each other's first names? Yours is Susan, I believe, and as you know, mine is Hannah. I expect to be back very soon, but, in case I'm delayed, please go ahead and have your coffee.'

Being left by herself gave Suzy a chance to examine her surroundings in detail. In addition to the bed and a built-in dressing table with clothes closets on either side—there was more storage in the lobby—the room was equipped with a writing table and desk chair as well as two comfortable armchairs with a coffee table between them, and the cupboard which doubled as a stand for the television.

The décor was in soft shades of khaki with blue accents. Double-glazing shut out the sound of the traffic which she knew must be streaming along Fifth Avenue although, without craning out of the window, she could not see it.

She found it hard to believe she was now in the heart of New York, with her family and all the people she had known from childhood more than three thousand miles away on the other side of the Atlantic. Later on, before going to bed, she would have to telephone her parents to let them know she had arrived safely.

But at this moment, sipping hot coffee and looking round her comfortable new quarters, far from feeling any twinge of homesickness, she felt more like a released prisoner who, after years of confinement, is at last free to make a fresh start.

This is what I should have done years ago, she thought. Even if they're in love, no one should marry at nineteen. What do they know about life . . . or the world . . . or anything?

Dad and Mother should have made us wait. Even if, legally, we didn't need their consent, we wouldn't have married so young if they had been opposed to it. And if we hadn't got married, Chris would still be alive.

As she looked across the room at the snub-nosed, boyish face of her husband, she could not help contrasting his features with the shrewd dark eyes and somewhat cynical mouth of the man who had brought her to America.

What had Wolfe Vyner looked like at twenty?

Probably even at that age his cosmopolitan background would have made him more mature than Chris, whose experience of the world beyond Yorkshire was limited to holidays in Majorca and Tenerife with his parents.

There was a third knock at the door. This time it was Hannah returning.

She said, 'By the way, Mrs Sawyer is the only person whose calls are put straight through to Mr Vyner's suite. All other calls are referred to me or, if I'm not available, the switchboard will check with him before they connect whoever is calling.'

She hesitated for a moment before adding, 'Mrs Sawyer and Mr Vyner are very close friends, and have been for a number of years You'll often see pictures of her in *W*, which is the fortnightly colour supplement published by *Women's Wear Daily*, the bible of fashionable America. They say there are now only about two thousand women in the world who have the means to buy all their clothes from the Paris couturiers. She is one of them, and always on the best-dressed list. She was married to a much older man who left her an extremely rich widow. I doubt she will ever remarry.'

She paused to put sugar in the coffee which Suzy had poured for her.

'This may sound like gossip, Susan, but it isn't intended as such. Because Mr Vyner's home is also his office, and there's no clear division between his public and private lives, it's important you're aware of the nature of his personal life. He doesn't live by the rules that govern the average person. In no sense is Mr Vyner average.'

'Someone in London called him one of the outstanding men of our time.'

'That's right—he is. Genius is a word usually applied to artists and composers, and no one thinks it strange if they live differently from the rest of us. But although Mr Vyner is a financial genius, people tend to be more critical of his unconventionalities.'

'Does he have other ... close friends apart from Mrs Sawyer?'

'Two others. One in England and one in Paris. Probably you've read about his friendship with Lady Belinda Stratton?'

Suzy shook her head. 'No, but she was at the Connaught Hotel when Mr Vyner interviewed me.'

'Yes, she usually comes to London when he's there. In Paris he lives at the Plaza-Athénée. His French friend is Madame Dupont. She and her husband separated some time before Mr Vyner met her. Those are his only relationships. Sometimes the columnists imply that he has other involvements but it isn't true. There are only three women in his life.'

'Do they ... know about each other?'

'Oh, yes, they know,' said Hannah. 'Everyone knows. Mr Vyner dislikes publicity and avoids it whenever he can, but no one in his position can escape it entirely. However, it's only when they have nothing new to write about that the columnists dredge up his private life and speculate which of his women friends may eventually become his wife.'

She leaned back in her chair and crossed her long thin legs. 'I've no doubt that when they discover he has engaged a young, attractive blonde to be his new secretary, they'll try to make something of it. They may call and try to trip you into making some indiscreet statement about him. So be careful what you say when you're speaking on the telephone to anyone you don't know.'

Aware of her weakness for unguarded answers, Suzy found this warning rather alarming.

She said, 'A propos the telephone, I should like to call my parents later. I take it that calls from this room will be charged to me, not to Mr Vyner?'

'No, all your expenses here, including your personal telephone calls, room service snacks, laundry, dry-cleaning and so on will be paid for by the Vyner Corporation. Free telephone calls are one of the rewards of the position—and it's no sinecure, let me tell you,' Hannah added, with a rueful smile. 'Most of the time Mr Vyner is a very easy man to work for. But not always. And if something annoys him—oh my!'

She flung up her hands in a gesture suggesting a cataclysm.

CHAPTER FOUR

By six a.m. the next day—mid-morning for people in England—Suzy was wide awake and longing to go out and start exploring.

As soon as it was fully light, she went down to the lobby, which was unexpectedly busy with early departees, and set out for a pre-breakfast walk.

Like London first thing in the morning, New York was quiet at this hour with, as yet, little traffic. First she walked east for a block, which brought her to Madison Avenue, both sides lined with fashionable shops.

She decided to cross the street and walk up that side for fifteen minutes, then return by the opposite sidewalk. But the window displays were so fascinating that, without realising how far she had come, she found herself ten blocks north. As she didn't have time to window-shop her way back, she turned left on 71st Street which brought her back to Fifth Avenue and the edge of the park.

She was about halfway to the hotel, when a voice behind her said, 'Good morning.' She turned to find her employer rapidly catching up with her.

'You're out early. Couldn't you sleep?' he enquired, as he drew alongside.

'I slept very well, but I woke up early and wanted to stretch my legs.'

'You should buy yourself a track-suit and come jogging with me every morning.'

He pulled off his sweatband, wiped his face with the end of the length of towelling which was tucked inside the collar of his track top, and raked back his springy dark hair.

'I don't think I could keep up with you,' she said. 'In fact I'm sure I couldn't.'

Even though he had moderated his stride, she was having to walk more briskly to keep level with him.

'Probably not, for a week or two. You'd soon get in condition. D'you know how to skate?'

'On rollers, yes. At least, I used to be able to as a child. I've never tried ice-skating.'

'There'll be ice-skating on the Wollman Rink from mid-October. It's in the park, a short walk from the hotel. Anyone with a sedentary job needs regular strenuous exercise—especially women.'

'Why especially women?'

'Because they're not conditioned to feel they ought to be fit, the way men are. As a sex, women have a poor body image. They think muscles are un-feminine.'

'Do you admire muscular women?' she asked curiously, thinking of Lady Belinda's opulent curves under the dark silk dressing gown.

'I admire healthy, active women with a spring in their step and natural colour in their cheeks,' he answered. 'I'm sure by the end of this decade our concept of beauty will have changed. In New York and London it already has to some extent. Exercise studios are proliferating. Even fashion models aren't as skinny as they used to be. They're looking like athletes rather than stick insects these days. The ideas promoted by women like Fonda and Principal may not have had too much effect in the Mid-West and the English provinces yet, but they will. Currently the leading manufacturer of leotards and exercise tights has sales of around one hundred million dollars, and I believe that market is nowhere near saturation. I've recently bought an unsuccessful clothing company and a factory making cheap footwear. I'm turning the first over to leotards and the factory is going to make running shoes in a better range of colours than any of the existing manufacturers. I've heard women complain they can't buy shoes to match their track-suits.'

Suzy realised she had never met a man who took this kind of interest in women. Certainly her father and her brothers-in-law didn't. Nor had Chris. They...

But she had no time to define their attitude to women before he went on, 'I was still at school and you were a baby when jeans came into fashion. They've stayed in for twenty years and a lot of people have made a lot of money from them. They could have been a passing fad. But they weren't. In fact I think there's still a lot of mileage in them, although maybe not another twenty years. With hindsight, it's never difficult to see why one trend lasted and another didn't. Jeans were linked to the revolution in which the young took over the purchasing power which had been in the hands of the middle-aged middle classes. They were also linked, in America, to the anti-Vietnam war effort. Those factors are easy to recognise in retrospect. What I have to do is make intelligent judgments about the future.'

'And you think the exercise cult is going to last?' she asked, looking up at him.

'I do. For one very good reason. It becomes an addiction, like cigarettes or alcohol or coffee. People become dependent on it. I know from my own experience that if I don't exercise daily I feel the same deprivation as a smoker who's run out of cigarettes or a drinker who's out of drink. Maybe my withdrawal symptoms aren't quite as uncomfortable as theirs but they exist.'

The creases in his cheeks deepened as he gave her an amused look. She was suddenly intensely conscious of the charm he could exert when he chose.

'You think I'm exaggerating, don't you?'

Suzy said, 'I have heard that some people get a "high" from running, but I thought that was mainly professionals . . . not everyone.'

'It can happen to everyone, if they exercise regularly and strenuously enough to get what's called "the training effect". What happens is that any kind of work-out, whether running in the park or exercising indoors, creates chemicals in the brain called endorphins which are thought to be stronger than morphine and equally addictive. The more people exercise, the more they want to.'

They had arrived at the hotel. One of the first differences Suzy had noticed between New York and London was that here many buildings had long canopies between the entrance and the roadway to protect people from getting wet as they crossed the sidewalk to cars and cabs.

In the elevator, Wolfe Vyner said, 'Come up to the suite at nine. I shall be out most of the morning, which will give Hannah time to show you around and explain her basic routine.'

Suddenly, to her astonishment, he took hold of her right arm, raising her elbow with one hand and placing the fingers of his other hand midway along her upper arm.

'Clench your fist and make a muscle,' he told her.

It took her a moment or two to overcome her surprise. Then she did as he instructed.

'Hm . . . if there's a bicep in there, it's keeping a very low profile,' he said, letting go her arm.

Before she could reply, the doors opened and he added, 'This is your floor.'

As she waited for her breakfast to arrive, Suzy repeated his test of the strength of her arm. With her hand tightly clenched she brought it slowly towards her shoulder. True, her upper arm didn't

bulge, but how many women's arms did? She
wondered if Mrs Sawyer was a paragon of physical
fitness.

She found out a few hours later when Mrs Sawyer
came to the suite to ask Hannah to make copies of an
agenda for a charity committee meeting for her.

'I meant to give this to Mr Vyner last night, after
the theatre, but I forgot and I need them by this
afternoon. Can you manage that for me, Hannah?'

'Certainly, Mrs Sawyer. This is Susan Walker, my
replacement.'

Mrs Sawyer acknowledged the introduction gra-
ciously but without Miss Eisenhart's warmth of
manner.

Evidently Mr Vyner liked variety. She was quite
different from Lady Belinda. Her short hair was
brown, worn in a mop of loose curls which, falling
forward and almost hiding her eyebrows, emphasised
her slanting blue eyes.

She was dressed in a beige cashmere suit with all the
hallmarks of Chanel, and the dark blue beads on one
of her neck chains were probably sapphires, Suzy
realised later on. Her skin was flawless, but the
delicate colour on her cheeks had been applied with a
blusher brush and it was impossible to imagine her
panting and sweating after strenuous exertion.

She looked as if her only exercise was stepping in
and out of limousines and walking across luxurious
carpets in her high-heeled glacé kid pumps. Suzy
doubted if Mrs Sawyer had ever lifted anything
heavier than a bowl of roses in her life.

'Is this the first time you've been in New York,
Susan?' she enquired.

'Yes, it is.'

'I'm told you won the title of Britain's Top Secretary.
Hannah is unquestionably America's top secretary. I

never knew anyone so quick and efficient. Thank you, Hannah, I'll pick those up later.'

Flashing her large but otherwise perfect teeth at the other woman, and giving the last of the smile to Suzy, she swept out.

'She didn't forget to give this to Mr Vyner. She wanted an excuse to give you the once-over,' Hannah said dryly, when they were alone.

Suzy wondered if she ought to mention that no one ever called her by her full name and she preferred the diminutive by which she had always been know. Then it struck her that perhaps Susan sounded more dignified.

'Does Mrs Sawyer often ask you to do things for her?' she asked.

'Almost never. She's the chairperson, as they say now, of this committee, not its secretary. I shouldn't be surprised if the secretary has already organised copies of the agenda and Mrs Sawyer has copied hers out by hand as a pretext for coming in here this morning. Of the Three Graces, as I call them, Dena Sawyer is the most possessive and jealous. She wouldn't have liked it had you been very glamorous. By that I don't mean to imply that you aren't nice to look at. You have a lovely face and a good figure. But you aren't the type to make bedroom eyes at Mr Vyner. He wouldn't have engaged you if you were.

'Nor is he the kind of employer to make your life difficult,' she went on. 'One reads a great deal about the sexual harassment of women employees, and I guess it does happen quite often. But although you'll spend a lot of time travelling with him, and staying in hotels with him, you have nothing to worry about on that score. I'm not saying that merely because he never made a pass at me when I was younger—I haven't got what it takes to attract a man of his calibre. But I've known him a long, long time. He would consider it unethical to take that kind of advantage of anyone on his payroll.'

'With three beautiful mistresses dotted around the world, I shouldn't think he feels much urge to pounce on anyone else,' said Suzy laughingly.

As she finished speaking, she knew by the expression on Hannah's face, and a prickle of awareness down her own spine, that they were no longer alone.

She turned. The door Mrs Sawyer had closed behind her was open and Wolfe Vyner was crossing the large living-room to the lobby which connected it with his secretary's office.

Had he heard her irreverent comment on Hannah's testimony on his behalf?

Her mouth dry, heartily wishing she had held her tongue, she watched him advance towards them, expecting a caustic set-down.

But if he had heard what she'd said, he chose to ignore it, and also to ignore her as he said to his retiring secretary, 'Give me the CATV file, would you, Hannah?'

When he had returned to the living-room, closing the heavy sound-proof door behind him, Suzy said anxiously, 'Do you think he heard what I said?'

'Probably, but I shouldn't worry about it. By the way, that CATV file is one you should study some time, Susan.'

'What is CATV?'

'Community Antenna Television ... what we usually call cable television. It's estimated that, by 1990, sixty per cent of all homes in the United States will go cable. Already it's a two-billion-dollar industry with projections for thirty per cent annual revenue growth.'

She went on explaining the industry's potential, and Suzy tried hard to concentrate and not to panic over

making a horrendous faux pas on her very first
morning as a cog in Wolfe Vyner's wheel.

Presently, having dealt with Dena Sawyer's agenda
on the word processor and put the copies in a large
envelope, Hannah asked her to take it downstairs so
that Mrs Sawyer's chauffeur could collect it from the
hall porter's desk.

On her way back from this errand, Suzy encountered
her employer. He walked out of the elevator she was
waiting to enter.

For an instant he checked his stride, as if he
intended to speak to her. Then, with an unsmiling
nod, he moved past her. Her heart sank. She felt sure
he was extremely annoyed with her but, perhaps on
his way to a business lunch, hadn't time to deal with
her now.

The suite had more than one entrance. There was
the main door, and the one used by Hannah and Suzy
and the hotel staff to come and go without disturbing
Mr Vyner.

At one o'clock a waiter brought them their lunch on
a trolley which opened into a table. Hannah had
ordered a delicious-looking pineapple and cottage
cheese salad.

'I always eat lightly at midday and have my main
meal at night,' she said. 'I used not to eat any
breakfast except several cups of black coffee, but Mr
Vyner persuaded me to change that bad habit. He
always eats a big breakfast and I do now, and feel
better for it.'

To Suzy who, back in Yorkshire, had taken a lunch
box to work, it was strange and very luxurious to be
seated at a damask-clothed table set with elegant
crystal and silver.

She said, 'Has he converted you to jogging? I met
him in the street early this morning and he told me I
ought to exercise.'

Hannah smiled. 'He tried to convert me, years ago, but I resisted. I'm not an inactive person. At weekends, I often walk miles, looking for subjects to photograph.'

'Oh, yes, I remember he mentioned you were a photographer and a needlewoman. He'd been asking me if I had some hobbies to amuse me when I wasn't working.'

'And do you?'

'Not at the moment. But, as I told him, exploring should keep me occupied.'

'Yes, it will. There's so much to see here. This evening, as soon as its dark, I thought you might like to walk down to the Empire State Building and see Manhattan by night from the eighty-sixth floor. It's the most fabulous view, which many New Yorkers never see. They think it's touristy, you know. But I take all my out of town friends there, and I never tire of it. After that we'll have dinner someplace. Do you like sashimi and sushi?'

'I don't know what they are?' Suzy admitted.

'Japanese cuisine. You either hate it or you love it. There are several good Japanese restaurants down on East 48th and around there.'

Mr Vyner did not return during the afternoon, and the consciousness of his wrath hung over Suzy like a cloud. She did not believe he was the kind of man who ever let pass anything which seriously displeased him, and she knew she should never have made that impertinent remark about his private life. It was not her place to comment on his lifestyle.

Yet she could not help feeling amazed that three beautiful, socially prominent women should allow themselves to be treated like concubines in an Eastern seraglio, taking turns to enjoy their lord's favours.

And, although they had to share him, she felt sure that he didn't share any of them, but expected complete fidelity, however long he might be absent.

Although she had never been an active feminist, the idea of any Western man—however rich, however personable—treating women like members of a harem was totally repugnant. How could he love all three of them? Obviously he didn't. They were no more than toys to him.

Yet she hadn't forgotten how, that night at the theatre with Alix, she had seen him kiss Lady Belinda's hand in an intimate and tender way which had sent a faint pang of envy through her.

It had been such a long, lonely time since she had been kissed or caressed; had felt a man's lips on her skin, a man's hand stroking her body.

Sometimes the longing for love came upon her like a sudden fever, keeping her awake at night, forcing her to an expedient which, although it eased her restlessness, left her unfulfilled emotionally, and depressed by the thought that this might be all she would ever have; this solitary, inadequate substitute for the ecstasies of a shared bed.

'Four o'clock. Time for tea,' said Hannah, making Suzy look up with a start from the book of instructions concerning the computer which was one of the many machines Wolfe Vyner had at his disposal.

Guiltily, she realised that for some minutes past she had not been reading but thinking. Thoughts which should not be allowed to enter her mind during working hours.

'Tea?' she said, raising her eyebrows. 'I didn't think Americans often drank tea.'

'I do—and I have some chocolate chip cookies from a batch which I baked last weekend for my prospective stepsons,' said Hannah. 'I've always loved cooking but rarely had the opportunity since my mother died and I gave up the apartment. Living in hotels, being waited on, is very nice most of the time.

But now and again you long for a place of your own. George—that's my husband-to-be—tells me I'll soon tire of cooking for him and the boys, but I don't think so. Did you continue working after you married, Susan?'

'No ... no, I didn't,' said Suzy. 'I ... I stayed at home until my husband ... died.'

She knew that to be widowed so young aroused people's sympathy and curiosity. Yet even now she found it difficult to talk about Chris in a natural way. Her intelligence might tell her that she shouldn't blame herself for what had happened, but in her heart she still felt an aching remorse that she hadn't been there that afternoon. The fact that Chris himself had urged her to go for a long walk, saying that Billy, his dog, needed more exercise, didn't lessen her lingering guilt.

The suite included a butler's pantry which was where Hannah made the tea.

'We'll have it in the living-room. Mr Vyner doesn't mind my sitting there when he's out. Sometimes we have tea together.'

Suzy had already noticed that the paintings which hung on his walls here did not include any nudes. They were all still lifes; not the gruesome arrangements of slaughtered game birds and dead hares which she had seen in museums and always disliked, but pictures of luscious fruit, or of bread and cheese beside a pitcher of wine.

Later that day she was in her room, changing to go out for the evening and wondering if it was caring for the late Mrs Eisenhart which had prevented Hannah from marrying when she was younger, when the telephone rang.

'Suz ... Susan Walker speaking.'

'Would you come up, please, Mrs Walker.'

The peremptory tone made her inside contract with foreboding.

'Yes, right away, Mr Vyner.'

But before she left the room, she made a hasty call to Hannah to say, 'Mr Vyner has just sent for me. I may be a little late meeting you.'

'Oh . . . well, thank you for letting me know. Instead of meeting in the lobby, why don't you come to my room when you're through upstairs?'

'Right . . . I'll do that.' Suzy hoped her voice didn't betray the panicky feeling within her.

Going up to the suite in the elevator, she forced herself to relax and take several deep, calming breaths. The man couldn't eat her, she told herself.

She had been given a key to the service door of the suite. She let herself in, crossed the lobby and, quaking, knocked on the door leading into the living-groom.

A curt voice responded.

'Come in.'

Most of the time Mr Vyner is a very easy man to work for. But not always. And if something annoys him—oh my!

When Hannah had said that to her yesterday, Suzy hadn't anticipated that about twenty-four hours later *she* would have annoyed Mr Vyner and be about to experience the meaning of that exclamatory *oh my*!

She opened the door and walked in.

He was standing half turned away from her, contemplating a picture of wild strawberries heaped in a Chinese bowl which Hannah had told her was by an eighteenth-century Dutch artist.

As he turned to face her, she saw that he was wearing a dinner jacket, the snowy collar of his dress shirt emphasising his tan.

Most men looked their best in evening dress, even her father and father-in-law, both burly, ruddy-faced countrymen with thinning hair and double chins.

Wolfe Vyner—his hair still thick and his jawline

taut—looked superb. Apprehensive as she was, Suzy
had a sudden flash of understanding why Mrs Sawyer,
Lady Belinda and the as yet unknown Madame
Dupont put up with the chagrin of knowing he was not
theirs exclusively. What woman wouldn't enjoy an
evening—even a night—with this princely man with
his brilliant mind and tall, strong, panther-lithe body?

But even as the thought shot through her mind, she
recognised that his expression held a grimness she had
never seen before.

CHAPTER FIVE

AFTERWARDS Suzy didn't know where she found the courage to take the initiative, instead of meekly awaiting a dressing-down.

Even more surprisingly, her voice was steady as she said, 'I know why you've sent for me, Mr Vyner. I owe you an apology. This afternoon I made a remark which I know was . . . very unbecoming. I assure you I don't make a habit of such indiscretions. It won't happen again. I'm sorry it happened today.'

It seemed a long time before he answered; endless moments in which his dark eyes held her fixed to the spot where she stood, awaiting his verdict.

At last he spoke. 'It's a rare and commendable trait to admit to error before being accused of a fault. Most people plead not guilty and, if possible, shift the blame to someone else,' he said dryly. 'I'll be frank with you, Mrs Walker. When I heard you make what you rightly describe as a most unbecoming remark before lunch today, I thought I'd been mistaken in my judgment of your character. There's no place in my team for anyone lacking discretion. What, may I ask, prompted that ill-judged remark?'

This time Suzy thought before she spoke. Unable to see how the truth could do any harm, she said, 'Hannah had been saying—quite unnecessarily—that I needn't have any fear that my job might involve . . . harassment.' She pronounced it in the American way with the accent on the second syllable instead of, as in England, the first.

'Why do you say "quite unnecessarily"?'

'I had never worried that it might. I don't know,

because it's never happened to me, but I should imagine that men who harass their female employees are either henpecked at home, or so unattractive they *have* to use duress,' she answered.

A hint of amusement lurked at the corners of his mouth.

'I see. I'm relieved to hear that you didn't seek that assurance from Hannah,' he said dryly. 'Is your room to your liking? Have you everything you need?'

'Yes, thank you. It's extremely comfortable.' Mindful that Hannah had made a reservation at one of the Japanese restaurants she had mentioned, she added, 'Tonight Hannah is taking me to see the view from the Empire State Building, and then she's going to introduce me to sushi.'

'New York has a splendid selection of the world's cuisines. Mexican . . . Chinese . . . Jewish . . . Italian— there's an *embarras de choix* of good things to eat. Enjoy yourself.'

Knowing she was free to go, she said, 'Thank you. Goodnight, Mr Vyner,' and quickly left the room.

It was only when she was back in the elevator that she felt the limp aftermath of tension. She knew she had been within a hair's breadth of being sent back to England.

On the day before Hannah left for Boston—where they would see her again when they went to her wedding—Suzy reminded her that she had promised to disclose some secrets about shopping in New York.

'They aren't really secrets. Most people know them, but not everyone makes use of them,' said the older woman. 'If you want to dress well on a budget, the trick is to look for your clothes in the top stores like Henri Bendel, Bergdorf Goodman and Altman's, but to buy them on the Lower East Side. The shops selling couture clothes on Orchard Street and Canal

Street don't display very much—they don't have the space. You have to take a list of what you want with the code numbers from the stores' price tags. They won't always be able to produce whatever it is you've made a note of, but when they do it will be much, much cheaper than the same thing bought on Fifth Avenue. And if you buy designer clothes, after you've worn them a few seasons, you can sell them at the resale shops where people like Jackie Onassis take their discards. That way you can dress almost as well as Mrs Sawyer for a fraction of what she spends.'

'What sort of clothes shall I need for the trip to Barbados?' Suzy asked.

While Hannah and her husband were on their way to Bermuda for their honeymoon, she would be accompanying Wolf Vyner to the Caribbean for one of his frequent working holidays.

'A couple of swimsuits, a beach wrap, two or three sundresses and something to wear in the evening if you're invited out,' advised Hannah. 'Barbados isn't strong on dress shops. I've only ever discovered one chic boutique there. It's at the Sandy Lane Hotel, and the prices are crazy. So don't count on buying your sun clothes there, as you can on some of the other Caribbean islands.'

Hannah's final and most startling piece of advice came on the day of her departure.

She said, 'I hope, for your own sake, you won't have this job as long as I've had it. But it is a wonderful job. You'll see a lot of the world and meet all kinds of interesting people. Just don't make the big mistake which I made in my first year.'

'What was that?' Suzy asked.

'Don't fall in love with your boss.'

Suzy couldn't hide her astonishment. 'You fell for Mr Vyner?'

'Fool that I was—yes, I did. You have to remember

I was only a little older than you are when I started
working for him. I had a nice boy-friend then, too.
But he didn't match up to Wolfe—very few men do.
Insanely, I let that friendship die of neglect. By the
time I came to my senses and realised I was sighing
for the moon, Tom was married to somebody else and
had a couple of kids. It took that long for me to wake
up to the fact that Wolfe isn't the marrying kind and,
if he were, he would want the female equivalent of
himself—someone with brains, beauty and breeding.'

She smiled as she added, 'I guess you're more level-
headed than I was in my twenties, and now he has a
different kind of private life. The Three Graces
weren't around then. He was playing the field. But
mostly he was busy establishing himself, and not all
his enterprises were successful in those days. We used
to work late four or five nights a week, and sometimes
he'd take me to supper and talk out his plans for the
future. It wasn't his fault that I fell for him. He never
gave me any encouragement except by being a
considerate employer and a very charming man.'

Suzy completed her three-month probationary period
on Pine Cay, an eight-hundred-acre paradise in an
archipelago of eight islands and forty cays in the blue
and sunlit Atlantic between the Bahamas and Haiti.

In recent years Pine Cay and its larger neighbour,
Providenciales, had become havens of relaxation for a
number of very rich people who considered the
Bahamas and most of the Caribbean islands to have
been overdeveloped and spoilt.

Here on Pine Cay there was only the Meridian
Club, a small colony of holiday houses owned by
people most of whom travelled in their private planes,
and a geodesic dome by the boat dock which was the
headquarters of the Foundation for the Protection of
Reefs and Islands from Degradation and Exploitation.

Her employer had come to Pine Cay at the invitation of a friend who had a house there and thought Wolfe should have one.

Nowadays, although she still called him Mr Vyner, she thought of him as Wolfe. He called her Susan, but as yet he hadn't suggested she should adopt Hannah's practice of using his first name in private and being formal only when other people were present.

On this trip, he could have left her in New York. There had been little for her to do except to transcribe some notes he had made with his pocket recorder while inspecting sites for new houses.

Apart from that, she had spent her time lazing in the sun and improving the tan which still lingered from the earlier trip to Barbados.

Late in the afternoon on the day which marked the end of her trial period, she was lying on her side on a sun-bed on the deck beside the Club's beautiful pool, the brim of a planter's straw hat shading her face from the still intense rays of heat, when she saw him coming towards her.

The sight of him, striding barefoot round the edge of the pool, each movement of his long legs displaying the powerful thigh and calf muscles developed by his daily run, roused her from her sun-induced lethargy.

She swung her feet to the warm paving slabs of the deck and hitched up the top of her bikini. Both pairs of strings were tied between her shoulder blades.

Rising, before he reached her, she said, 'Do you want me for something, Mr Vyner?'

'Only to tell you that we're flying out tomorrow morning. I've just heard something on the radio which makes me want to get back to civilisation—or uncivilisation, as Bill calls it.'

Bill was his host, an American multi-millionaire who had wearied of sophisticated resorts.

'Are we going to New York?' she asked.

'Yes, for a few days. While we're there, remind me to deal with your contract. That's assuming you feel, as I do, that the test run has been satisfactory.'

Suzy did not disguise her pleasure. Although he had a phenomenal memory, she hadn't expected the date she had started working for him to have lodged in his mind.

'From my point of view, more than satisfactory,' she answered. 'How many secretaries enjoy all this?'— with a gesture encompassing the thatched sun-shelters, the sea-grape bushes, the fine white sand and shimmering viridian sea.

'All this is fine for a week, but I shouldn't care to spend months here as some of these people do,' he said, glancing round at the people sitting in the shade and the glistening bodies stretched out in motionless sun-worship. 'Maybe in twenty years' time I'll be ready to join the lotus-eaters, but not yet. See you later.'

She watched him walk down to the lagoon, his broad shoulders tapering to narrow hips, the whole of his back rippling with muscle. She sighed, wishing he had said, 'I'm going for a swim. How about you?'

She remembered Hannah's warning. *Don't make the big mistake I made in my first year. Don't fall in love with your boss.*

It had been too late even then. She knew now she had fallen in love with Wolfe Vyner that first day in London.

That night they went to a party at which Suzy met a Frenchman named Robert Marigny. At first his manner towards her was no more than polite. When he discovered she was Wolfe's secretary he became much more attentive.

'I thought you were his girl-friend,' he told her.

'What is the significance of this?'—touching her wedding ring. 'You are divorced?'

'I'm a widow.'

'For how long?'

'Three years.'

'Your husband was much older than you?'

'Only a year.'

'Oh, to die young is very sad. But in three years the heart recovers. You have now a lover?'

His directness startled and amused her. She shook her head.

'But why not?'—with a very Gallic lift of the shoulders. 'You are young and beautiful. You should have a lover. Can't you find a man you like?'

She said lightly, 'Not so far, but I haven't been looking very hard. At the moment I'm in love with New York. Have you been there?'

'Many times. I've been everywhere.' He pushed back the lock of fair hair which had fallen forward across his forehead. His eyes were blue-grey. Although he had only arrived on Pine Cay a few hours earlier, his skin was not white.

'What is your profession?' Suzy asked, to divert his interest from her life.

'I'm what we call a *bon vivant*. What is that in English? A sybarite?'

'Yes, but it isn't a profession.'

'*Au contraire*, it is a most exacting profession. To enjoy every day . . . to fill every hour with pleasure is not at all easy.'

'I should have thought it impossible.'

'Not for me. I will admit that some days go better than others. Tomorrow is going to be one of my very best days. I am going to spend it with a lovely girl to whom I am much attracted. In the morning we shall borrow a boat and sail up and down the lagoon. In the afternoon . . . *celà dépend*.'

For a moment or two Suzy thought he was talking about someone else. As it dawned on her that he meant her, and that he had said 'it depends' in a tone which left little doubt how he hoped to spend the afternoon, she could not stop herself blushing.

Robert took one of her hands and kissed it. 'What time shall we meet? At sunrise?'

She withdrew her fingers from his. 'Mr Vyner and I are leaving Pine Cay tomorrow.'

'Oh, that's too bad. Where are you going?'

'To New York.'

'Then I also must come to New York. Not right away, but soon. Do you believe in destiny?'

Suzy smiled at him. 'I suspect that your destiny has involved quite a lot of meetings at sunrise, Robert.'

He smiled back at her. 'There have been many women in my life—I admit it. But each time I hoped it would be what you call "the real thing". Love is like everything else . . . it's only by trial and error that one arrives at perfection. Shall we dance?'

Long ago, in that other life before the accident, her first act after waking in the morning had been to switch on the radio and find a station playing dance music. She had danced round her bedroom while brushing her hair, danced on the spot in the bathroom while brushing her teeth, and danced down the stairs to breakfast.

Her father, driven mad by pop music, had given her a transistor with a headset so that he didn't have to listen to the music which set her feet tapping. Two or three times a week she and Chris had spent the evening at a disco. They had been listening to pop on the radio of the sports car which Chris's parents had given him for his twenty-first birthday at the time of the accident. After that there had been no more music, and no more dancing.

So it was with a good deal of reluctance that she let

Robert steer her on to the floor. At first her movements were awkward, like those of a person with no natural sense of rhythm.

But the Frenchman was an excellent dancer and the music, although unfamiliar—nowadays her taste was for opera and orchestral music—had a catchy beat. She began to relax, the forgotten pleasure reclaiming her, her hips swaying, her shoulders lifting.

The numbers, playing off a tape, followed each other with only a few seconds' interval. They danced to three lively recordings before there was a change of tempo.

By this time, so long out of practice, she would have been out of breath but for the exercise classes which, during the past two months, had improved her physical condition.

Wolfe's strictures about keeping fit had spurred her to enrol at a work-out studio.

'They say you can tell from the way a woman dances how she will make love,' Robert murmured, as he started to take her in his arms.

But as his arm circled her waist, a bronzed hand fell on his shoulders and Wolfe said coolly, 'There are other people who would like to dance with Susan, Marigny. You can't expect to monopolise her all evening.'

It was a situation in which Robert had no choice but to relinquish her to the taller man. As she changed partners, Suzy was aware of a pulsing excitement she had not felt moments before.

However, Wolfe did not hold her close as Robert would have done. His right hand resting lightly on her waist, he said, 'You seem to like dancing.'

'I used to love it, when I was in my teens.'

'What do you think of Robert Marigny?'

'He's obviously a tremendous flirt.'

'He's more than that,' he said dryly. 'Getting women into bed is a sport with him.'

'I suppose that could be said of most men at some stage of their lives.'

'Of young men—yes. Marigny is twenty-nine or thirty. He's a bad type.'

He widened the space between them in order to look down into her face.

'And if you're thinking that some people might say the same of me, there's a difference. My women have never included other men's wives or inexperienced girls. Anyone is fair game to Marigny.'

'Well, thank you for warning me, but I don't think I'm in much danger, particularly as we're leaving here tomorrow.'

'Just so long as he doesn't persuade you to go for a moonlight stroll with him. I'm told he's a very fast worker.'

'So he may be—with easy conquests. I don't happen to be one,' Suzy said, a little stiffly.

Again he drew back to look down at her. 'Have you had any dates since you started working for me?'

Unwilling to admit that she hadn't, she said, 'I've been out to dinner two or three times.'

Obviously this surprised him. He said, 'You have? Not with any of my people?'

By now she had come into contact with most of the men who advised him, and a number of senior executives in charge of the American companies which were part of his empire. A couple of them had invited her out. Knowing them to be married men, she had politely refused.

She said, 'No, with friends I've made outside working hours.'

'Where?'

'Really, Mr Vyner, I don't think that's any of your——'

'You can call me Wolfe when we're off duty.'

'If you wish; but on or off duty I don't think you have the right to cross-examine me about my personal life.'

'New York isn't Yorkshire. I credit you with a lot of commonsense, but perhaps not the worldly know-how to recognise an undesirable acquaintance. Any friendship which starts with a pick-up, even if it happens somewhere like the Frick Collection, has an element of risk in it. Have you been to the Frick yet?'

'Yes.'

The mansion, built during the first world war by a Pittsburgh coke and steel industrialist, Henry Clay Frick, was a few blocks north of the Pierre. Suzy had been there one Sunday afternoon. Within five years of building the mansion, Frick had died and left the house and its contents—at that time the finest private collection of art in America—to the people of New York City.

'You noticed the organ beside the staircase with the pipes on the landing, I expect?' said Wolfe. 'On Saturday afternoons, Frick used to hire an organist to play the pop music of the day to him while he read the *Evening Post.*'

'Really? The afternoon I was there I heard a young man tell his girl that Frick's fortune was founded on the blood of workers who were killed when they went on strike for a union contract.'

He shrugged. 'Some people say the Rockefeller millions are tainted with the blood of miners. But John Davison Rockefeller who, when he was fifty, was the richest man in the world, was also a great philanthropist. He gave six hundred million dollars to medical research and other good causes. We're getting away from the point, which is how and where you met your dinner dates.'

'If you must know, they were all women . . . women I've met at my evening classes.'

'What kind of classes are you taking?'

'Exercise classes.'

'I thought you looked fitter than you did when we were in Barbados. Your swimming has improved and you walk with more spring in your step.'

'Thank you.' She was surprised he had noticed. She had seen him appraising other women's figures, but he'd never looked at her in that way, or not when she was aware of it.

'Perhaps you should take up tennis,' he said thoughtfully. 'It's a good way to make social contacts with people of both sexes.'

'For the time being I'm perfectly happy with friends of my own sex.'

'Are you? Why?' he asked, with that disconcerting directness.

She considered the question. She always thought before she spoke now. The truthful answer was: Because I've fallen in love with you. Even though nothing can come of it, other men don't interest me.

She said, 'Because I don't think it's possible for men and women to be friends, except perhaps when they are both happily married and have some special interest in common—either their work or a particularly absorbing hobby.'

'Yes, I'd go along with that,' he agreed. 'But there are other relationships beside friendship.'

'Yes—affairs with men like Robert. I'm not interested. I prefer to concentrate on my job and absorbing other kinds of experience.'

The music stopped, and he released her. A moment later she was claimed by their affable host for a duty dance.

She had no further private conversation with Wolfe that evening. Nor, rather to her surprise, did Robert single her out again.

Perversely, because she had had her own doubts

about him before Wolfe's warning, she went to bed
slightly disappointed that after making a set at her he
had later sheered off.

Ten days after their return from Pine Cay, Suzy
returned to her room at the end of the day to find a
vase of apricot carnations on the coffee table.

At first she thought they must have been put
there by mistake. But as she was about to call the
hotel florist and point out that someone else's
flowers had been delivered to her, she noticed a card
in the foliage.

On it was written—*Important you call me. I shall be
at this number from 5—7.00 p.m.* Then a telephone
number and the initials R.M.

For a second or two they meant nothing. Then she
remembered the Frenchman who had told her she
should have a lover and proposed himself. He had said
he would come to New York, but in the meantime she
had forgotten him.

How had he found out where she was? Through
their hosts at Pine Cay, presumably. Clearly it wasn't
really important for her to call him. But for the
flowers, she could have disregarded the message. For
all he knew, she might be busy between the times he
had stated.

However, the extravagant flowers—three dozen of
them—put her under an obligation at least to thank
him.

When she dialled the number, it turned out to be
that of the Mayfair Regent Hotel on Park Avenue at
65th, which was only a short walk from the Pierre. She
had passed the place more than once, and had also
made reservations for Wolfe to dine at Le Cirque, the
Mayfair Regent's renowned French restaurant.

She was not put through right away. After giving
his name to the operator, she was asked for hers.

Was that hotel policy, she wondered; or did Robert like to know who was on the line before accepting a call? If Wolfe's allegations were true it could be that the Frenchman had to take care to avoid his past loves.

'Suzanne . . . how are you?' On the telephone his accent seemed more pronounced.

'Very well, thank you. And you?'

'All the better for hearing your voice. It's been too long since we danced, but I couldn't get here any sooner. Did you believe me when I told you I should follow you here?'

'Not really . . . and I'm sure your main reason for coming to New York is something much more important than looking me up,' she said lightly.

'You're wrong. I have no other reason than to see you. When can we meet? Tonight? Are you free to have dinner with me?'

'I'm afraid not.'

'You have a date with someone else?'

'No, I have an evening class.'

'Can't you play truant for once?'

'I don't want to. I enjoy my classes.'

'What are you studying?'

'Anatomy.'

'You're an artist in your free time?'

'No.'

'Don't tell me you're studying to become a nurse. They had better not put you in charge of any male patients. Excitement isn't good for men with weak hearts or high blood pressure.'

'It's healthy anatomy I'm studying. How to develop long flexible muscles and ligaments.'

'You want muscles? You must be crazy! You already have a beautiful body—why do you want to spoil it? Muscles are for men.'

'Brains used to be for men once. Now it's recognised that we have them, too.'

'My God! Don't tell me I've fallen in love with a feminist!'

'Oh, Robert, don't be absurd. You haven't fallen in love with me. And I'm not a feminist—or only when a man says something like you just did. By the way, thank you very much for the flowers.'

'I was going to send you red roses, but then I saw the carnations and they reminded me of the colour of your skin when I made you blush,' he said caressingly.

'I wish you hadn't been so extravagant,' she told him.

'What time does this muscle class finish? You'll be hungry after all that exercise. I'll meet you and feed you on steak, or whatever strong women eat.'

'I shan't be suitably dressed for the kind of places you dine at.'

'You don't know where I like to eat. I know plenty of restaurants where no eyebrows will be raised at a pretty girl in a leotard. Do you also wear leg-warmers?'

'No.'

'You should, they are *très érotique*. What is the address, and what time shall I fetch you?'

Why Suzy decided to capitulate, she had no idea. She knew Wolfe would disapprove if he ever found out. She knew Robert's motive for pursuing her could only be sexual conquest. She knew she was a fool to begin something which she had no intention of ending in the way he had in mind.

Yet, with all those reasons to refuse him, she found herself giving him the address of the exercise studio, and telling him what time to be there.

He took her to a Hungarian restaurant on Second Avenue. It was small and not particularly elegant. On the way there in a cab Robert had told her the food was all home-made and excellent.

'Why aren't you wearing your leotard?' he asked, helping her to remove her raincoat.

'I usually change to walk home.'

She didn't explain that by the end of forty minutes of strenuous exercise, her long-sleeved black leotard and those of her classmates were invariably drenched with sweat. Fortunately the studio had showers. She had piled her hair inside a cap and spent three minutes under a downpour of hot and then cold water. Now, in a cream silk shirt and black wool crêpe skirt, she could have dined almost anywhere without looking out of place.

'You walk home? At night? Is that safe?'

'It seems to be. I'm never out late and I don't go down any dark side streets. What brings you to New York?'

'I told you—you do.'

Suzy smiled at him. 'But I didn't and still don't believe you.'

A waitress brought them two menus. 'Good evening. May I get you a cocktail while you order?'

'What would you like to drink, Suzanne?' Robert enquired.

Evidently he meant to continue using the French form of her name. 'A glass of red wine, if I may?'

'I'll join you. May I see the wine list?'

The waitress had it with her. Robert studied it briefly, made his choice and, when she had gone to fetch it, said, 'Nevertheless it's true. I have no other reason for being here. I wanted to see you again. Why is that so hard to believe? The reason is in your mirror every time you look at your reflection. You're beautiful.'

'Thank you,' Suzy said politely. 'But, at the risk of sounding ungracious, I'd better tell you that it takes more than three dozen carnations, a delicious dinner and some flattery to get me into bed. If you're expecting to end the evening making love to me, I'm afraid you'll be disappointed. Casual sex isn't my scene.'

Far from looking annoyed, he seemed amused. 'Do you say this to everyone who takes you out to dinner?'

'The situation hasn't arisen before. You're the first man I've dined with since my husband died.'

The smile died out of his eyes. After a pause, he said quietly, 'You must have loved him very much.'

Instead of saying, 'Yes, I did,' she found herself saying, 'I don't know. We were both very young and immature. I'm not sure that people of that age are really capable of love. Have you ever been married, Robert?'

'No. As somebody said, marriage is a great institution, but I'm not ready for an institution yet.'

The waitress came back with the wine, her return reminding them they hadn't yet studied the menu. As Suzy had never had Hungarian food before, she asked Robert what he recommended.

'I suggest we start with the marinated herring, and then have the chicken *paprikash* with *nokeldi* pasta and sour cream sauce. Does that sound appetitising?'

'Delicious!'

When the waitress had left them, he asked, 'How long have you worked for Wolfe Vyner?'

'Just over three months.'

'I could tell by the way he cut in when we were dancing that he wanted to break it up. I've met him in Paris several times. He disapproves of me. I expect he told you to steer clear of me.'

'Yes, he did.'

'But you've decided to ignore his advice.'

'I like to make my own judgments about people. But I don't think he would have told me you had a bad reputation with women if there wasn't some truth in it.'

'His own reputation isn't spotless. Do you know about his women?'

Suppressing her curiosity about Madame Dupont, whom Robert probably knew, Suzy said, 'I never discuss Mr Vyner, and that was a red herring. It was your reputation we were talking about.'

He shrugged. 'Okay, I'll admit I've been around. But all women aren't angels, you know. Now that they don't have to worry about getting pregnant, most of them do what they like. There aren't many virgins over the age of sixteen. They want to find out what it's all about, and why not? Having sex isn't a crime. It's one of the good things of life.'

Suzy said thoughtfully, 'I wouldn't know, but I should have imagined having sex with someone you didn't love was about as good as synthetic cream.' Then, wanting to change the subject, 'Do you spend a lot of time in Paris?'

'In spring and autumn I enjoy Paris very much. In summer there are too many tourists. In winter the weather is impossible.'

'We're going to Paris later this month. I've never been before. I'm looking forward to it. What are the things I should see first?'

'On your first night in Paris you must have dinner with me under the vine at La Colombe. It's the oldest bistro in Paris, on the Ile de la Cité, the island in the Seine. On the other island, the Ile St Louis, which is smaller, I have my apartment which, one day, I'll invite you to visit. It's a very nice place to live; in the heart of Paris, but peaceful. The house was left to me by my grandmother, who was a friend of Vyner's grandmother. Did you know he was one-eighth French?'

She nodded.

'It's a large house, so I had it converted into four apartments,' he went on. 'I have what used to be the attics for the servants. They were made into one very big room, and I also have a roof garden with a view of the river. The rents from the other apartments allow me to live as I please.'

'They must be very high rents if they cover staying at hotels like the Mayfair Regent,' she remarked, still suspecting that it was some kind of business which had brought him to New York.

'They are high. The Ile St Louis is a most desirable place to live. President Pompidou used to live there. Most of the houses were built in the seventeenth century when French architecture was very fine. All the principal rooms in my house have beautiful painted ceilings. Unfortunately Grand'mère would never agree to the conversion. Consequently she spent the last years of her life with very little money and only one maid to look after her, instead of being comfortable.'

'Does Mr Vyner's grandmother also live on the island?' Suzy asked.

'No, she has an apartment at Passy on the west side of Paris, by the Bois de Boulogne. It's in the same block as Jacqueline Dupont's apartment. She's your boss's French mistress—a very convenient arrangement. It allows him to combine duty with pleasure.'

Suzy made no comment on this piece of information. 'Before your grandmother died, did you have a job then?' she asked.

He grimaced. 'Don't remind me! I was in banking—an extremely boring occupation from which I was delighted to resign.'

'Was there no other career which would have interested you?'

'No, I always wanted to be a man of leisure like my grandfather and his father. They weren't expected to work.'

'But now, when everyone works, isn't it rather

lonely being the last of an outdated species? What do you find to do with yourself if your life is a perpetual holiday?'

'Many things. I travel. I enjoy several sports ... skiing, windsurfing, sailing and so on. I have friends everywhere from Palm Springs to St Tropez. Somewhere there's always a house party which, as an unattached man, I'm welcome to join. I am never bored now, I assure you. Would you expect to be bored if you could resign from your job?'

'I don't know. Perhaps not.'

When they had finished their chicken, Robert persuaded her to share some *palacsintas* with him.

'You must try them,' he insisted, when Suzy protested that she'd already had a large meal. 'They're like our *crêpes*, or what you and the Americans call pancakes.'

Each with a different filling of apricot butter, sugared walnuts and cottage cheese, the Hungarian pancakes were very good. Knowing that her work-out would counterbalance the calories, Suzy ate her share with enjoyment.

At home she had kept her slim figure by not eating the cakes and desserts which made her mother a stout woman and her sisters plumper than they should be. But since starting her exercise classes, she had lost several pounds.

'Tomorrow we might try an Indian *thali*, or perhaps some Greek food,' Robert suggested, as they finished dinner with coffee and a plum brandy called *slivovitz*.

'But I can't dine with you again tomorrow night,' she said hastily.

'You have another engagement?'

'No, but—but you must have friends in New York who would like to see you.'

'Some of them I can see during the day while you're working. I would rather spend my evenings with you—even if I can't persuade you to have breakfast with me,' he added, with a quizzical smile.

He took her back to the Pierre by cab, asking the driver to wait while he walked her to the door and kissed her hand. He didn't say any more about seeing her the following evening.

As she crossed the lobby, Suzy was conscious that from the moment the taxi had drawn up outside the hotel she had been worried about running into Wolfe. She did not feel relaxed until she was safely in the elevator going up to her floor.

CHAPTER SIX

WHILE she was having breakfast the next morning, the telephone rang. It was Robert. He wanted to know how she had slept, what she was eating for breakfast and if she would meet him for lunch.

'No, I'm sorry I can't,' she said firmly. 'I only have half an hour.'

'Only half an hour—but that's barbarous! The man is a slavedriver!'

'On the contrary, he's a very considerate employer. How many secretaries can have poached salmon or Châteaubriand for lunch if they choose?'

'Don't have Châteaubriand today or you won't have room for an Indian *thali* tonight. I'll call for you at seven—yes?'

Against her better judgment, Suzy agreed.

He continued to chat until she was forced to say, 'I must ring off now, Robert, or I shall be late.'

'Okay, I'll pick you up at seven. *À bientôt!*'

But she didn't see him that evening because by midmorning she and Wolfe were on a plane to Toronto. In the message she left at Robert's hotel, she didn't say where they were going, but merely that it was unlikely they would be returning to New York for some time.

Suzy had been working for Wolfe for seven months before she went home for the first time—and discovered that her parents' house in Brockthorpe was not her true home any more.

She had become, like her employer, a citizen of the world; more at ease in New York and Paris than in the small Yorkshire town where she had grown up.

It was an illuminating visit, for it showed her, more clearly than she had realised, how much she had changed and developed.

'Had a good time?' Wolfe enquired, when she rejoined him in London.

'Yes, thank you.'

But in fact she was glad to be back. Her long weekend in the north, while he had been staying with friends on the Isle of Wight, had been a disappointment and, if she were honest, a bore.

Her association with him had stretched her mind and broadened her outlook beyond measure. She could never revert to the person she had been before, nor did she want to.

From London they flew to Brussels and then to Paris, where Suzy made the arrangements for a dinner party to celebrate Wolfe's grandmother's seventy-ninth birthday. She had met the old lady several times and knew that she doted on Wolfe, although she tried not to show it. She had faded but still shrewd blue eyes. Sometimes she made Suzy nervous that she might detect how her grandson's secretary felt about him.

It was on another visit to Paris that she ran into Robert again. She was strolling under the covered arcades of the Place des Vosges, the most beautiful square in the city, when someone exclaimed 'Suzanne!' and she turned to find Robert beaming at her.

They had dinner together that night; and for the rest of her stay he paid assiduous court to her. But on her last day in Paris, while they were sitting in a pavement café, he said to her, 'I'm not getting anywhere with you, am I, *chérie*?'

They both knew what he meant. She liked him and enjoyed his company, but she was never going to sleep with him.

She shook her head. 'I'm afraid not.'

When, after they had had dinner, he escorted her
back to the Plaza-Athénée, she knew she was unlikely
to see him again. There was no place in Robert's life
for platonic friendships, and no place in hers for casual
affairs.

It was from Hannah that she learned that Wolfe's
'harem' had been reduced to two.

She had asked him for a mid-week day off so that
she and his former secretary could go shopping
together. Hannah and her husband, George, had
arrived in Manhattan the previous afternoon. Suzy
had gone to the theatre with them and, afterwards,
taken them to dinner.

Next day George had things of his own to do, which
left her and Hannah free to arrange an early
rendezvous at Bloomingdale's department store—
which Suzy was now enough of a New Yorker to call
Bloomie's—for a day of woman-talk and window
shopping.

'How's the shopping in Boston?' asked Suzy, as they
started by wandering around the store's designer
boutiques.

'Now I'm getting to know my way around, not
bad. I've already had some great bargains from
Filene's basement. You must come over and we'll
have a poke around together. Quincy Market has
some nice shops. But Boston's not like New York. It
has more of a small town feeling. You don't see that
kind of elegance,' said Hannah, turning to admire a
beautifully dressed fellow browser who had just
strolled past them.

'Do you miss New York?' Suzy asked.

'Oh, no—no, not for a minute. Well, maybe for ten
minutes sometimes,' Hannah corrected herself, smiling. 'I'd hate never to come here again, but I wouldn't
want to live here any more. But I guess that's not

because Boston is nicer than this city. It's because of my lovely new lifestyle.'

She slipped her arm through Suzy's and gave it a friendly squeeze.

'I adore being a *hausfrau*. I don't miss working at all.'

'I should think, with George and the boys to look after, you're working as hard, if not harder, than you ever did when you were here.'

'Maybe so, but somehow it's different, working for yourself. It used to be Wolfe who set the schedule. Now I do. Talking of Wolfe, what happened with him and Dena Sawyer? Have you any idea what caused the break-up?'

'I didn't know there'd been one. Are you sure?'

'As ever is. It must have happened some time ago. I picked up the news from an old magazine at the hairdresser's. It seems Dena has been seen wining and dining with someone else. She wouldn't be doing that if she and Wolfe were still like that'—crossing her second finger over her forefinger. 'You make his reservations, and order the flowers and the jars of fresh Royal Beluga which he used to send her instead of chocolates. You should know when he ditched her.'

'You're right. It is quite some time since I organised any of those things. I assumed she was out of town for a few weeks. Maybe she's ditched him,' Suzy suggested.

'You have to be joking! Ditch Wolfe?'

'Perhaps she got tired of sharing him.'

'My guess is he got tired of her trying to nudge him towards the altar. I wonder who will replace her? You may not know for some time. At the beginning he chooses the flowers himself, and the presents. They only show up on his charge accounts.'

However, as time went on it seemed that Mrs Sawyer was not going to be replaced.

One of Suzy's regular tasks was to clip and file newspaper items which Wolfe had ringed with red pencil.

A technological development in which he took a keen interest was the conversion of water into liquid hydrogen fuel for aircraft and automobiles. When perfected, so he had told her, this was going to have a revolutionary effect on the world economy, although it wasn't likely to make a significant change for at least two decades.

Late one afternoon, she was clipping a report of an important announcement from a scientific team at the Texas Agricultural and Mechanical University, when he came into her room and asked, 'Are you free tonight, Susan?'

It was the night of her exercise class, but she said, 'Yes.'

'Someone I know has arrived in town unexpectedly and wants me to have dinner with him and his wife—his third wife. She's almost thirty years younger than he is and she hasn't a brain in her head, or none that I've ever discovered. I wonder if you would mind making up a foursome and letting her prattle about clothes to you? Otherwise I shan't get any intelligent conversation out of him, and, except in his choice of wives, he's a very intelligent man.'

'I'd be delighted,' she said. 'What time do you want me to be ready?'

'They're arriving here for drinks at seven. I didn't ask him where he'd booked for dinner, but if it hasn't a dance floor, we'll be going on to a nightclub later. His wife is mad about dancing and Boris indulges her every whim. You like dancing, too, I remember.'

'Yes,' Suzy agreed, thinking that the cotton evening dress she had worn at the party on Pine Cay wouldn't do for a New York nightclub. 'Will it be black tie?' she asked.

'No, but Charlene will dress to the hilt. She always does. I expect she'll wear something extremely décolleté to show off her principal assets and Boris's latest love token,' was his sardonic reply.

'Oh, dear. I haven't got much of an evening wardrobe. A silk shirt would look too covered-up, I suppose?' She glanced at her watch. 'Perhaps, if you don't mind my leaving this filing until tomorrow, I should dash round to Bloomie's and get myself something more suitable.'

Wolfe didn't immediately agree, but seemed to consider the question. Finally, to her astonishment, he said, 'I'll come with you.'

If he wanted to supervise her choice, she could hardly refuse to allow it. Five minutes later the doorman was asking, 'A cab for you, Mr Vyner?'

Wolfe said, 'No, thanks. We're not going far.'

They turned south towards Grand Army Plaza, the square at the corner of the Park where the horse-drawn carriages waited to take tourists for drives through the green oasis between East Side and West Side.

But when Suzy would have turned east along 59th, Wolfe took her by the elbow and continued straight down Fifth Avenue until, two blocks on, he crossed to the west side of the street and she realised they were heading for Henri Bendel which, with Bergdorf Goodman, was one of the two most elegant stores in Manhattan, the kind of place where very rich socialites shopped.

'Oh, but Wolfe, I can't buy a dress here,' she objected, as they approached the entrance.

'Why not?'

'This store is outside my budget.'

'But not outside mine.'

She stopped dead. 'I can't let you pay for a dress for me.'

'Don't be silly,' he said impatiently. 'You don't object to my paying your air fares.'

'That's different.'

'Not at all. Tonight I want you to do something outside the normal range of your duties. You have nothing suitable to wear, so it's up to me to provide you with something.'

'But I could find something perfectly suitable and much less expensive at Bloomingdale's.'

'I haven't an account there. Come on. In less than an hour they'll be closing.' Again he took her by the elbow and marched her briskly inside the store.

As she stood in front of him on the escalator, gliding slowly up to the fashion floor, he said, speaking into her ear from the step immediately behind her, 'I shan't introduce you as my secretary tonight. Charlene is intimidated by any woman brighter than herself, and that upsets Boris. Do you mind playing the part of someone equally feather-brained for one evening?'

His breath was warm on her cheek. Half-turning her head, she answered, 'Not in the least. But what shall I say if she asks me about my job?'

'I doubt if she will. She'll chatter non-stop about herself. If she asks you anything, it will be the name of your nail varnish or where you have your hair done.'

'If your friend is a clever man, how can he stand a wife who's as dim as she sounds?'

'He didn't marry her for intellectual companionship. He's a self-made man who got his first leg up by marrying the boss's plain daughter. She died, and his second wife was a very astute businesswoman who helped him consolidate his success. Charlene is his pleasure-wife. She makes him feel young and virile. He likes looking at her, but I shouldn't think he ever listens to her.'

'Isn't he afraid that she might leave him for a younger man?'

'She likes being an old man's darling. Her eyes never stray in the direction of any younger men. She gets her kicks in Van Cleef & Arpels,' said Wolfe, referring to the famous jewellers they had passed a few minutes earlier.

Suzy had wandered round Henri Bendel's before, but the saleswomen had seemed to sense that she wasn't a potential customer. Now that she was escorted by Wolfe, they eyed her with greater interest.

When one of them came forward and said, 'Good afternoon, Mr Vyner. May we help you?' he said, 'We're looking for something suitable for dining and dancing.'

'Certainly.' The saleswoman cast an experienced eye over Suzy's figure before asking, 'Had you any special colour in mind?'

Suzy said, 'Black.'

Wolfe said, 'Red.'

'Red?' she repeated, in a startled tone. It was a colour she had never worn.

'Red,' he affirmed. 'Not bright red. Dark red. The colour of pink sapphires.'

She hadn't known there were such things as pink sapphires.

Probably the saleswoman hadn't either, but she didn't show it. She said smoothly, 'If you'd like to sit down, I'll bring a selection for you to see. Size eight?'

Suzy nodded. Wolfe sat down and crossed his long legs, much more at ease than she was. He hadn't convinced her it was right for him to incur this expense. Admittedly he could afford it, but it went against the grain with her to pay designer salon prices when, given more time, she could have found something suitable in Ohrbach's down on West 34th, a store which specialised in cheap copies of high fashion styles.

To buy quality clothes for day wear was a sensible

investment. But she felt evening things were different.
They weren't worn as often and, in the soft lighting of
restaurants and the semi-gloom of discos, who would
notice the difference between silk and polyester
chiffon, real silk and silky-look fabric?

Afterwards, she suspected that it had been a
deliberate technique on the saleswoman's part to
return with five or six dresses, all of them exceedingly
chic, but none of them red.

'Unfortunately we don't seem to have this lady's
size in the colour you asked for, Mr Vyner. My
colleague is checking through, but meanwhile you
might like to see some of these on. This soft blue is
lovely with blonde hair,' the woman suggested.

Suzy tried on four of the dresses. None of them felt
right to her, and Wolfe didn't approve of them either.

Each time she emerged from the fitting-room, he
took one look and shook his head. She began to feel it
was her fault the dresses didn't please him. On Dena
Sawyer they would all have looked stunning, and
presumably it was with Mrs Sawyer that he had come
here before, often enough for some of the staff to know
his name and accord him the special deference given
only to the very rich.

She was about to try on a fifth dress when they were
joined by another saleswoman, carrying a dress of dark
pinkish red silk chiffon.

'Oh, you've found the colour, Mrs Miller. But I
thought that Halston had been sold,' said the first
saleswoman.

'The customer sent it back. Her husband didn't like
it. I thought she was too heavy for it. It does call for a
very good figure.'

'This lady has a lovely figure, so I'm sure it will suit
her perfectly, and the colour is exactly what Mr Vyner
wanted,' Suzy's assistant said enthusiastically.

On the hanger, the dress didn't look anything

special, apart from the vibrant colour and the beautiful filmy fabric.

She should have been warned when the saleswoman suggested she remove her bra because the dress didn't need one. Obediently she took it off and allowed the dress to be put over her head.

It was lined with silk crêpe-de-chine that slithered over her bare skin with a softness which she had to concede was quite different from the feel of polyester.

She had her back to the mirrors while the saleswoman did up the fastenings. The sleeves were unlined, the waist tight, the skirt close-fitting over the hips but full at the knee-length hem. It wasn't until she turned to see her reflection that she realised how much of her bosom was exposed by the low V neckline. At least a third of each breast was on view.

'Oh, this isn't my style at all,' she exclaimed emphatically. 'No, definitely not!'

The fitting-room was close to where Wolfe was sitting. He must have heard what she said.

His deep voice, slightly raised, said, 'Come out here and let me be the judge of that.'

'I thinks it looks lovely on you,' said the saleswoman.

She propelled an uneasy Suzy into the showroom.

Fingering the edges of the neckline in an attempt to hide her uncovered curves, she stopped a few yards from his chair.

He gave her a brief inspection before saying, 'Turn round: let me see the back.'

A telephone rang somewhere nearby. 'Would you excuse me for a moment?' The saleswoman hurried away.

'Now the front again,' said Wolfe. When she turned back to face him, he added, 'Put your hands down.'

Reluctantly, she did as he told her, her colour rising as his dark gaze took in the deep V.

'It's excellent,' he told her. 'Your colour, your style
. . . perfect. Have you any suitable shoes?'

'I've some black patent sandals.'

'High heels?'

'Medium high.'

He shook his head. 'Gold would be better.'

The saleswoman came back. She beamed when he
told her to charge the dress to his account and pack it
for them to take with them.

'I'll be having a look round the shoe department
while you're changing,' he said to Suzy. 'What size do
you take?'

'An American seven.'

When she joined him in the shoe salon, he had
already picked out a pair of Italian evening sandals for
her to try. They had much higher heels than she had
ever worn before, even in her giddy teens.

'Those are fine,' he told the assistant when Suzy
had walked back and forth in them. 'Is there a bag to
go with them?'

There was: a slim gold kid envelope.

'And a pair of sandalfoot pantyhose . . . the sheerest
you have,' he said, after approving the bag.

The saleswoman from upstairs was waiting for him
to sign the bill.

She said, 'If I may suggest, sir . . . a lipstick to go
with the dress? It's quite an unusual red, but I'm sure
our cosmetic department will be able to match it.'

It was five minutes to closing time when they left
the store; Wolfe carrying the dress box and the parcel
containing shoes and bag; Suzy clutching the smaller
package containing a Lancôme lipstick and a bottle of
Magie noire which he had insisted on buying for her.

The Pierre Hotel had five shops; a news-stand, a
florist, a barber shop, beauty salon, and the
Manhattan branch of Bulgari, the Roman jewellers
founded in 1881 by a Greek silversmith, Sotirio

Bulgari, and now world-renowned for fine work-
manship and striking design.

When they returned to the hotel, instead of making
for the elevators, Wolfe said, 'I imagine you would like
to have your hair done?'

'I usually do it myself. I doubt if the salon here
would be able to take me without an appointment.'

'They'll take you,' he assured her confidently. 'I
think you should wear your hair loose tonight. It'll be
quicker to have it done professionally than to tackle it
yourself.'

However, although he was right in thinking that for
someone under his aegis anything seemed to be
possible, he didn't leave her in the salon to have her
hair done immediately.

First he swept her off to the jewellers' shop. Suzy
often looked at the elegant adornments on display,
and she knew that a good-looking, blue-eyed man
she had seen leaving and entering the shop was
Nicola Bulgari, a grandson of the firm's founder and
now head of the business in New York. However, he
was not there. They were attended to by an elegant
older woman.

To Suzy's amazement, Wolfe said, 'I wonder if you
could lend Mrs Walker something to wear this
evening?'

'Certainly, Mr Vyner.' She had noticed the box
under Wolfe's arm. 'Is it to go with a new dress?
Perhaps if I might see the colour and style? It is
always much better when clothes and jewels comple-
ment each other.'

The dress had been packed with the bodice
uppermost. It wasn't necessary for Suzy to remove it
from the box for the woman to see the neckline.

'How does this appeal to you, Mrs Walker?' she
asked, showing her a necklace of pearls, each pearl
separated by a deep red bead, with a large oval-shaped

convex red stone surrounded by pavé-set beads and pearls as a pendant.

'It's gorgeous,' she said breathlessly, wondering what it must cost. 'Are they rubies?'

'No—pink sapphires. The cabochon'—indicating the oval stone with the tip of her little finger—'is just over eighteen carats and a very fine colour. An excellent match with your dress, wouldn't you agree? By the way, Mr Vyner, we have another *padparadschah* for you to see next week, if you're here. If you aren't, we'll put it aside for you.'

'I expect to be here.' Wolfe turned to Suzy. '*Padparadschah* is the Singhalese word for lotus flower. In Sri Lanka they have what's known as the sacred lotus. It's a beautiful apricot colour. The stones which Mr Bulgari is collecting for me take their name from the colour of that lotus.'

'The finest of all *padparadschah* is across the park in the Morgan Memorial Hall at the Natural History museum,' said the jeweller's assistant. 'Have you seen J. P. Morgan's collection of jewels, Mrs Walker?'

Suzy shook her head, although she had heard of John Pierpont Morgan, the multi-millionaire banker, yachtsman and collector.

'Tiffany's gemologist assembled a collection of outstanding stones for him, including the Star of India and the Midnight Star. You should go and see them,' said the older woman.

'Dangerous advice,' Wolfe said dryly. 'I took it and lost my heart to the *padparahschah*, the least popular member of the sapphire family. Bulgari is one of the few jewellers who will handle it.'

'It isn't a sapphire which appeals to the nouveau riche buyer, or the buyer who thinks only in terms of investment,' the woman agreed. 'It's a gem for the connoisseur who responds to the beauty of a stone. Are you happy with this necklace, or shall I show you some others?'

She addressed the question to them both, but Suzy left it to Wolfe to answer her.

He said, 'This will do splendidly.'

'Would you like some ear-rings? The pearls Mrs Walker is wearing are a little small in relation to the pearls in the necklace.'

And whereas those in the necklace were either real, or the finest cultured pearls, those in her ears were not even cultured—a fact which her expert eye had undoubtedly recognised, Suzy thought.

'Right: you go and have your hair done,' Wolfe told her, after the jeweller's assistant had produced a pair of pearl ear-rings more in keeping with the necklace.

'I'll take care of the jewellery, and I'll also stop off at your floor and ask one of the maids to unpack and hang up your dress. Come upstairs at ten to seven.'

Relieved that she was not to be responsible for the safety of what she felt must be thousands of dollars' worth of jewellery, Suzy returned to the beauty salon.

As the shampooist washed her hair, Susy wondered if Wolfe was buying the rare *padparadschah* sapphires merely to have a unique collection of them, or, if, eventually, he would commission the jeweller to design a fabulous ornament for one of the women in his life.

But would a man give such rare jewels to a woman to whom he had no lasting commitment?

Not that any commitment could ever be said to be permanent in a world where divorce was a commonplace. But somehow she had the feeling that, if ever he did marry, it would be for the rest of his life.

The thought that he might be collecting the lotus-coloured gems to adorn the future Mrs Vyner—a girl carefully selected to bear the heirs to his fortune—sent a stab of something like panic through her.

She knew that, if the day came when Wolfe

announced his engagement to some radiant society beauty on this or the other side of the Atlantic, she wouldn't be able to go on working for him. It would put an end to her daydream that one day he might look at her and see, not his unobtrusive capable amanuensis, but someone essential to his wellbeing.

As with most daydreams, she knew there was very little likelihood of it ever becoming reality. But, loving him, she had to have some hope to cling to. Lady Belinda and Madame Dupont she could accept. A wife she couldn't. Once he had a wife, he was lost to her for ever.

Her hair was too long and thick to be blown dry. It was set on the largest rollers and she was put under a hood and given some glossy magazines. Luckily she had given herself a manicure the night before, and her nails were at their best.

Later, seated at her dressing table, she took extra pains with her make-up, smoothing a transparent film of foundation over her fine, clear skin before setting to work with blusher, eye contour pencil, shadow sticks and mascara. The stylist at the salon had brushed and finger-combed her hair into a silky aureole of waves and loose curls, quite unlike her usual smooth, pinned-back styles. Carefully, she painted her mouth with the pink-sapphire lipstick. It had a creamier texture than the brand she normally used, sliding over her lips and leaving them glossy and luscious.

The scent bottle had a glass dipstick. Naked but for a pair of panties, she stroked perfume behind her ears, round the base of her throat, in the crooks of her elbows and underneath her small, firm breasts.

At Pine Cay she had not worn a monokini like some of the other women there; those accustomed to the topless sunbathing now commonplace in most of Europe. Two small triangles of paler skin showed where she had worn a bikini top, but they wouldn't be visible when she was dressed. She had noticed that when she was trying the dress on.

She put some *Magie noire* behind her knees, and stroked the dipper along the inside of her thighs, up one side and down the other. She had never scented herself as lavishly before, nor had she ever used French scent. In a family like hers, in rural north Yorkshire, women used inexpensive colognes and flower-scented talcs, not costly, seductive essences such as this one, chosen by Wolfe after the girl at the perfume counter had sprayed some on Suzy's left wrist and another fragrance on her right wrist.

Although not having to do any housework had made her hands softer and smoother than they had been when she lived at home, to be on the safe side she drew on a pair of kid gloves before putting on the gossamer pantyhose.

The high-heeled gold sandals flattered her ankles and legs. She practised walking around in them. Then she rang for a maid to help her do up the dress.

The one who came was a middle-aged woman called Mary with whom Suzy sometimes chatted.

She said, 'My, that's a beautiful dress you're wearing tonight, Mrs Walker. You going somewhere special?'

'Out to dinner, but where I don't know yet.'

'Maybe when your date sees you looking so good, he'll take you to the Four Seasons. That's where a lot of the folks who stay here go for dinner. There you are, ma'am.'

'Thank you very much, Mary.' Suzy slipped a tip into the pocket of the maid's uniform.

'Thank *you*, Mrs Walker. Have a nice evening.'

Suzy had no evening wrap, but recently she had replaced her pale beige Marks & Spencer raincoat with a more elegant black one made of some light but showerproof fabric which looked like silk.

Since becoming an habituée of some of the finest hotels in the Western world, she had noticed that not all rich women wore furs in the evening. Some wore velvet capes or brocade jackets, or even double-life shower coats such as her own. Perhaps they had scruples about furs, or perhaps it was a matter of taste since, in her observation, very often the most opulent furs were flaunted by women and girls whose style she did not admire.

As she took the elevator up to her employer's suite, she was conscious of butterflies fluttering inside her. It was excitement rather than nervousness which caused the sensation. She couldn't remember ever looking forward to an evening with greater anticipation, not even to the Young Farmers' Club dinner dance which had ended, as she had hoped it would, with several passionate kisses in the car when Chris drove her home.

Everyone had said how pretty she had looked, even though at seventeen she had been at least ten pounds overweight, with a perm which didn't really suit her and a dress which, in retrospect, had done nothing to camouflage her over-plump hips and thighs.

Now, many years older and wiser, she knew that tonight was as near as she would ever come to beauty. How Wolfe had known that red was her colour she couldn't imagine. Certainly she hadn't known it. Until today she would have said that anything red would be too overpowering on her. Instead of which it gave her impact and sparkle.

She let herself into the suite by the service door. It was eleven minutes to seven when she tapped on the inner door and heard him call, 'Come in.'

She remembered the day, more than a year ago, when she had been summoned before him and only her ready apology had saved her from losing her job before she had properly begun it.

Now, as she hesitated before opening the door, she felt a different kind of trepidation.

When she entered, Wolfe, who had a glass in one hand, was bending to help himself to an olive from a dish on a low coffee table. He was wearing a new suit, or one which she hadn't seen before.

He bought his country tweeds in England, his sports kit in France, his summer casuals in America, and most of his suits were tailored for him by Gregorio Luzzi, president of Rome's Accademia Nazionale Sartori, an association of master tailors, founded in 1575, whose present-day clientèle included presidents, kings, film stars, orchestral conductors and many other distinguished men.

Few could make a tailor's task as easy as Wolfe did, she thought admiringly.

He straightened, turning to look at her. As she walked across the spacious room, his dark gaze did a slow scan which began with her feet and worked upwards. But it wasn't the impersonal scrutiny he had given her the first time they met, and on other occasions since then. There was nothing impersonal in the way his gaze paused and lingered on her legs, hips, waist and bosom.

By the time she had reached the other side of the coffee table, he had reached her face and her hair. For the first time since she had known him, she saw in his eyes the sudden hot gleam of desire.

At last he was seeing her, not as a useful assistant, but as a woman; a woman he wouldn't mind having.

'I hope you approve of the hairdo.'

'Very much. I approve of . . . everything.' His glance flickered over her mouth and down to the curves of her breasts. 'What can I get you to drink?'

'Have you any cassis?'

'I not only have it, I have some Cassis de Dijon by l'Héritier Guyot.'

'Then I'll have a Kir, if I may?'

This was a French apéritif which Robert had introduced her to: half a jigger of cassis, a blackcurrant liqueur from Burgundy, topped up with chilled white wine or dry white vermouth. The drink, he had told her, had been invented by a priest who had also been Mayor of Dijon and a hero of the Resistance in the second world war.

Wolfe put down his glass, ate the olive and set about making her drink. Seeing the bubbles in the glass he handed to her, she thought he had used sparkling wine until he said, 'This is a Kir Royale, made with champagne.'

'Thank you.'

She took a small sip. She knew she would have to be careful how much she drank tonight.

'Shall I fasten the necklace for you?'

It was lying in its case on the table. He lifted it from its velvet bed and, standing behind her, lifted it over her head.

The pendant slid down the valley between her breasts. The pearls were cool on her skin, but his fingers were warm against her nape as he fastened the sapphire-studded clasp.

It was the first time he had ever touched her, except to shake hands. She trembled inwardly, wishing he would put his hand on her shoulders, turn her round to face him, kiss her.

Instead he picked up the case containing the earrings and offered them to her. Suzy put down her glass and took a pearl in each hand. She walked away to a mirror with an engraved portrait of George Washington in the *eglomisé* frieze above the glass.

She knew now that, as well as paintings, Wolfe collected antique mirrors. This one was a recent acquisition; early American with the original glass which, although misted and speckled by time, added greatly to its value and its beauty in the eyes of the cognoscenti.

As she fitted the fine gold posts through the tiny holes in her lobes, she wondered how many woman before her had used the mirror on very special nights in their lives. She wished she could ask Wolfe to take a photograph of her. She would never look like this again, with the lustrous Bulgari pearls making her skin appear golden in contrast to their snowy sheen.

The telephone rang. He answered it.

'Would you ask them to come up, please.'

She moved away from the mirror. As she returned to where he was standing, she saw him looking at the glowing cabochon sapphire in the centre of her revealing décolletage. Then their eyes met; in his, still, the glinting light which acknowledged her desirability.

As she picked up her drink and took another token sip, she knew that if, later tonight, he made a pass at her, she wouldn't resist him.

A plan which would scandalise her family, Alix, Hannah, everyone who knew her, was beginning to form in her mind.

CHAPTER SEVEN

BORIS Kashevsky was a short, balding, overweight man whose young wife was six inches taller than he. This was partly because she was wearing extremely high heels. Even without them she must be able to look down at him, thought Suzy, during the introductions. She wondered why Charlene Kashevsky didn't play down the disparity in their heights by wearing moderate or low heels. Perhaps Boris didn't mind being dwarfed by her. In spite of his unprepossessing appearance, he had an air of great self-confidence.

As they shook hands, she saw him taking note of her jewels, her designer dress, and her face, hair and figure. She wondered if he thought she was Wolfe's new amour in America; the successor to Dena Sawyer.

Almost immediately the men began to discuss the announcement about liquid hydrogen fuel and, without attempting to listen, Charlene turned to Suzy and complimented her on her dress.

'Who designed it?' she asked.

'Er . . . Halston.'

'Is he your favourite designer?'

'I wouldn't say he was my favourite. I like several American designers,' Suzy answered, with truth. 'Anne Klein . . . Geoffrey Beene . . . Betty Hanson. I also like the Italian designer, Laura Biagiotti, very much. Who is your favourite?'

'I guess I like Yves St Laurent best, and just lately I've been buying a lot at Valentino.'

Charlene was wearing a clinging one-shouldered slither of black lamé with assymetrical bands of black velvet and silver beading. The skirt was slit to above her black-stockinged knees. Small waterfalls of diamonds cascaded from the lobes of her ears. More diamonds glittered on her wrists. On arrival she had shrugged off a white mink blouson which now lay over a chair.

Watching her sip a Pink Vodka, her full lips leaving a smear of colour on the rim of the glass, Suzy was reminded of Wolfe's reference to her as Boris's pleasure-wife.

She wondered why he had married her when he could have made her his mistress. Perhaps marriage had been Charlene's price for surrendering her opulent body, and Boris had wanted her badly enough to give in to her. But the fact that they were married didn't lend any dignity to their alliance. It must be obvious to everyone that money was the only thing which held their relationship together.

As Charlene chattered about clothes and Suzy contributed a comment here and there, she wondered if she might be judging the other girl too harshly.

Perhaps, like the majority of her sex, Charlene had dreamed of loving a man when she was younger, but something had happened to turn those youthful dreams sour.

After all, a few years ago what I have in mind at this moment would have been unthinkable, thought Suzy, sipping her champagne.

Suddenly, in a stupendous flash of enlightenment, a few moments before the Kashevskys' arrival, she had known that although it might be contrary to her parents' code, and to her own received ideas, there was no reason why, if he wanted her, she shouldn't give herself to Wolfe.

The fact that he didn't love her was less relevant than her love for him. Somehow she had to give expression to that love. If she didn't, she would always regret it.

Whatever the aftermath, she knew that even one night in Wolfe's arms must enrich her life beyond anything she had or ever would experience. It was even possible that, although she would never be his wife, and only briefly his woman, she could come out of the affair with something far, far more precious than the sophisticated gifts he bestowed on his other mistresses.

She might become pregnant. Which, in her case, would not be a cause for dismay but rather for rejoicing.

Of course if such a thing happened it would have to remain her secret. But she had enough money put by to support her while she had the baby, and for some time afterwards. Later she would have no trouble in finding another well-paid post. One-parent families were a commonplace now, and she had the advantage of being entitled to call herself Mrs. If she stayed in America, no one need ever know the child was not the posthumous offspring of her marriage.

Her family would know, and it would be bound to upset them. But she couldn't allow that to influence her. She had to lead her life her way. She was irrevocably in love with Wolfe Vyner, and if she could never be his wife the next best thing was to be the mother of his child.

'Ready to go, girls?' asked Boris.

He took them to Quo Vadis on East 63rd Street. Suzy had sometimes made reservations there for Wolfe. She knew it had long been one of New York's legendary restaurants which, although recently revitalised by a new management, still catered to patrons who preferred classic dishes to any of the more recent developments in French cuisine.

The elegance promised by the marbled and mirrored entrance was fulfilled by an interior in the grand manner; a painted ceiling, wine-coloured velvet banquettes, immaculate napery and silver, and a well-trained staff under the watchful supervision of a suave *maître d'hôtel*.

They were shown directly to their table where Boris ordered champagne to drink while they studied the menu. Charlene seemed more interested in who else was dining there than in choosing what she wanted to eat.

'You decide for me, honey,' she purred, stroking his broad, hairy wrist with the tips of her fingers. She had very long, false, silver nails.

The way she looked at him and touched him made Suzy realise there was no reason why her own attitude towards Wolfe shouldn't be considerably warmer than usual. She could always fall back on the excuse that she'd thought it part of her role to flirt with him.

She turned to him, smiling, letting her admiration show. 'You've been here before. What do you recommend?'

He was quick to recognise the change in her expression and tone of voice. Amusement flickered in his eyes as he answered, 'The sweetbreads *en brioche* are very good.'

'What are sweetbreads?' asked Charlene.

'The thymus and pancreas glands of lambs or young calves. They have a very delicate flavour,' Wolfe explained to her.

Her lips made a moue of distaste. 'I don't like things like that.'

'Have you tried them?'

'No, but I know I shouldn't like them.' She turned to Boris. 'What's the name of that *pâté* I like? I'll start with that, if they have it.'

'Sure they have it. Whatever you want, they have it. It's *pâté de foie gras*. Do you like *pâté*, Susan?'

'Yes, I do—all except *foie gras*.'

Charlene said, 'Really? How strange. It's my favourite.'

Suzy was tempted to reply that perhaps Charlene didn't know about the cruel force-feeding which fattened the livers of the geese, but she changed her mind, saying only, 'I'll try the sweetbreads.'

When the men had made their decisions and Boris had studied the wine list, they resumed their separate conversation and Charlene asked Suzy where she had come by her sun-tan.

'I never sunbathe,' she confided. 'It's not good for your skin. It can give you premature wrinkles, even if you use a sunscreen.'

This led to a long discourse on the creams and lotions she used, had tried in the past and found wanting, and intended to try in the future. Obviously she thought of little else but her appearance, and Suzy wondered what would happen to her when her looks began to go off. Perhaps by that time she would be a wealthy widow, but not a very merry one, Suzy surmised.

After the sweetbreads she had poached turbot with courgettes fried in butter and wild mushrooms. The delicious food compensated for the dullness of Charlene's conversation. Fortunately, as Wolfe had forecast, she showed no interest in Suzy's background.

Several times during the meal she allowed herself the pleasure of gazing at him. When he noticed her watching him, instead of flicking her glance back to Charlene, she gave him the best she could manage in the way of a smouldering look.

She felt increasingly reckless, and it wasn't what she was drinking which made her feel that way; she was lifting her glass to her lips half as often as Charlene, and taking only small sips. It was the decision she had made which was intoxicating; the sense of being in charge of her own destiny.

From the restaurant they went to a club which, Charlene assured them, was the newest 'in' place. It was dark, with a small, crowded dance floor on which couples were doing a slow shuffle to music by a five-piece band.

'This kind of dancing I like,' said Boris, as soon as they had been shown to a table and he had ordered yet more champagne. He steered Charlene towards the floor.

'Would you like to dance?' Wolfe enquired.

She nodded. The thought of being in his arms had been making her weak at the knees all the way from the restaurant.

At the edge of the floor she turned to him, waiting to be drawn into the embrace she had imagined so often. He slipped his right arm lightly around her. The size of the floor and the number of people moving on it made a close embrace a necessity. It was no place for people who disliked each other; but neither was it essential for Suzy to nestle against him as she did. She couldn't see his facial reaction because she had her head on his shoulder, but the way his arm tightened round her waist and his other hand closed over her hand suggested that, even if it surprised him, he had no objection to her melting against him.

For her part it was the most thrilling sensation of her life to feel the hard breadth of his shoulder supporting her arm, the long muscular thighs pressing lightly against her slim legs. She wanted it never to end.

Later she danced, once, with Boris who quizzed her a little about her connection with Wolfe, but was easily diverted into talking about his visits to Europe.

Sometimes all four of them sat out a dance, but the noise level made conversation difficult and for most of the following hour they were on the floor.

The music didn't allow her to cling to Wolfe all the time. During the fast numbers she surprised herself.

She had always loved moving her body to music, but tonight she had no inhibitions; each rhythmic twist of her shoulders and supple swing of her hips was a deliberate invitation. She wanted to make him want her, and judging by the way he pressed her against him when the band changed tempo, she was succeeding.

Not having her watch on, she had no idea what time it was when Boris said, 'I don't burn my candle at both ends the way you do, Wolfe. Charlene and I are going to call it a day, but you people don't have to leave if you feel like staying till they close. That won't be for another three hours.'

Charlene looked disappointed. 'Couldn't we stay a while longer?'

'Uh-huh, honey. I'm ready for bed.'

Wolfe tilted an eyebrow at Suzy. 'I'm happy to leave now if you are.'

For answer she opened her bag and took out the cloakroom ticket for her coat.

Boris asked the driver of his car to drop his guests at their hotel before taking him to the Plaza. Charlene was looking sulky. Clearly she didn't want to break up the party.

As the car slid away from the kerb outside the Pierre, Wolfe raised his hand in a wave, then curved it round Suzy's elbow as they walked under the canopy and into the hotel. She wondered if he would invite her up for a nightcap, giving her a chance to chicken out.

The decision was taken out of her hands when, in the elevator, he pressed the button which would take them up to his floor.

Pretending not to have noticed, Suzy looked down at her feet, her inside in knots with excitement.

The lift doors slid open. She stepped out, wondering if he would expect her to show surprise—

or at least to simulate it—at finding herself in the foyer outside his suite.

Trying to keep her expression as inscrutable as his often was, she waited for him to unlock the door and feel for the switches which lit the lobby and a couple of lamps in the living-room.

There she put down her evening bag and began to unfasten the pearl ear-rings. Perhaps he would think that she thought he had brought her up here in order for the jewels to spend the night in his safe rather than in an unlocked drawer in her bedroom.

Wolfe didn't offer her a nightcap. He crossed the room to the music centre, opened one of the drawers where his large collection of tapes was stored, and spent a few moments selecting one and putting it on.

She didn't recognise the music, but it certainly wasn't the kind she would expect Robert Marigny to play when he took a girl back to his penthouse on the Ile St Louis.

This was a classical piece, played on a harp, the delicate tinkling notes interspersed with sweeping glissandi; a complete contrast to the throbbing beat of the music they had danced to in the night club.

'Would you like some help with the necklace?' he asked, coming back towards her.

'Yes, please.' She turned her back to him.

His fingers were warm on her skin as he dealt with the intricate catch. When it was undone, instead of removing the pearls from around her throat, he rested his hands on her shoulders, close to her neck, so that the pendant slid lower between her breasts.

The next thing she knew was that he was kissing her neck, his lips soft but his face no longer as smoothly-shaven as it had been when they set out. The masculine roughness of his chin and cheek sent a long, slow shiver down her spine. She stood transfixed while the warm mouth moved lightly over her nape.

Considering the effect it was having on her, it was amazing she was able to react when, suddenly, Wolfe let go of the necklace. She just managed to trap it against her and save it from falling to the carpet. As she did so, his long lean fingers slid caressingly outwards to take hold of the tops of her arms and turn her towards him.

She had a brief glimpse of his dark face before he bent his head and instinctively she closed her eyes to receive his lips on her mouth.

It had been so long since she was kissed that it was like the very first time. Almost as if he knew that, his kiss was unexpectedly gentle.

The hot gleam she had seen in his eyes was kept under control during those first moments in his arms. It was not until she was beginning to adjust to the strangeness that his hold on her became more masterful, his hands moving from her arms to the small of her back where they drew her more firmly against his tall, powerful body.

With her hands trapped between them, still clutching the Bulgari pearls, she felt his mouth lift from hers. But she didn't open her eyes, and seconds later he had plunged one hand in her hair, tilting her head back while he kissed a slow path from her chin to the pulsating hollow at the base of her throat.

Suzy gave a soft gasp of delight, her whole body relaxing and yielding as he gathered her even closer to him. When he found another soft pulse spot behind the lobe of her ear, she had to stifle a groan at the exquisite pleasure the touch of his mouth there induced.

How could she have lived for so long without these delicious sensations? When, softly, Wolfe bit the tender flesh of her lobe with his strong white teeth, her legs seemed to turn to jelly. She felt that if he hadn't been holding her, she might have collapsed, so powerful was her reaction.

Presently he stopped the amorous nibbling of her ear. She realised he had raised his head and must be watching her.

Her breathing as rapid and her heartbeat thudding as fast as if she had just done her work-out, Suzy lifted her lashes, half expecting to see a glint of sardonic amusement in the dark eyes looking down at her.

But for once his lean face held no mockery. He had his deliberating look; the expression he wore before an important decision. She had seen it too often not to recognise it, even though, this time, it was combined with the unfamiliar signs that he, too, was aroused.

She knew she was flushed. She could feel the hot blood in her cheeks. But she hadn't expected to see that his colour had risen. His eyes had a strange burning light, almost frightening in its intensity.

'Are you sure this is what you want, Susan?' His voice was thicker than usual.

She didn't hesitate. 'Yes.'

But fervent as it was, her affirmative didn't seem to satisfy him. Still he bent that deep, searching look on her upturned, excited face.

'You've had a good deal of champagne ... more than you're used to.'

'You don't think I'm tipsy, do you?'

'Not tipsy—no. But not quite cold sober either.'

She wriggled her trapped hands higher, taking the pearls in her left one and touching his cheek with the other.

'I wanted you to hold me like this *before* we went out with the Kashevskys. I'm not a young girl, Wolfe. I'm a grown-up woman. I know what I'm doing.'

Yet inwardly, she felt very daring as her fingers left

his hard cheek and explored the thick, springy hair brushed back from his temple.

'Yes, I guess you are. Although sometimes——'

He left the remark unfinished as her hand pulled his head down to hers and her lips parted, not to interrupt him but in a silent invitation.

This time his kiss was not gentle. As his mouth moved possessively on hers, she felt the stiffening of his body and a softening, dissolving sensation between her own trembling thighs.

The kiss seemed to go on for ever. But at last, reluctantly, he stopped it and, sweeping her feet from the floor, lifted her high against his chest. As easily as if she were a child, he carried her to the room she had never seen, his bedroom.

Having shouldered the door shut, he set her down on her feet and said, in a low voice, 'Stay where you are for a minute.'

She expected him to switch a light on, but he didn't. He left her standing in the total darkness of the unknown room. It wasn't until she heard the swishing of the curtains and saw the impenetrable blackness giving place to the magical panorama of Manhattan by night that she realised he had found his way to the windows.

Above the myriad golden lights of the city, the sky was alive with the cold platinum pinpricks of the stars. There was also a pale waning moon.

Now she was able to make out a vast king-size bed, neatly turned down on one side; the outlines of several deep chairs facing that magical nightscape; and, returning to where he had left her, the tall silhouette of the man who would soon be her lover.

When he reached her, he drew her against him and she leaned her head on his shoulder while he found the tag of her zipper and slowly unfastened her dress, his fingers caressing her spine until it would open no further. Then he peeled the dress carefully from her shoulders and eased her arms out of the sleeves until, with a slithery rustle, it fell to her feet, leaving her slim body naked to the waistband of her pantyhose.

In a bright light she would have been shy of being seen almost naked while he was still fully dressed. But the dim silver light of the moon made her feel less selfconscious as she stood in his shadow, wishing she had Charlene's voluptuous curves. Would her body disappoint him? Would he think her small, round breasts were too small?

Taking her by the hand, Wolfe led her round the huge bed to the side where it had been turned down. Bending, he took hold of the sheet and with one powerful jerk of his wrist flung the clothes to the foot of the bed. Then he sat down and pulled her with him, on to his lap, his strong hands caressing her waist before sliding higher to stroke and fondle the softer flesh.

Suzy managed to stretch out her arm and drop the pearls on the night table before, with a convulsive shudder, she buried her face against his neck, her slender hands clutching his shoulders as she felt all her normal controls being swept away by a tide of violent emotion.

'Take my tie off for me, will you?' he murmured huskily.

Her fingers made clumsy by the things he was doing with his hands, she fumbled to loosen the knot and then to unbutton his collar and, the tie pulled free and discarded, the other buttons of his shirt.

'Now kiss me,' he ordered softly.

The long kiss which followed, combined with his skilful caresses, sent her senses reeling. Slowly he lowered her torso until she was lying on her back with her head on a pillow and her legs still stretched across his lap.

'Shall I get rid of these?'

It was a rhetorical question. He was already peeling off her tights and, with them, her bikini-sized panties.

Through half-closed eyes, she watched him remove her gold sandals and toss them on to the carpet, to be followed by the tights and briefs. Then, starting at her instep, his warm hands retraced their path, gliding sensuously under her calves; lingering at her knees to touch sensitive places behind them which she hadn't known existed; sweeping with tantalising slowness back to the top of her thighs . . . and then down . . . and up . . . and down again, until her breathing was ragged and soft skin below her navel was fluttering from the tension inside her. When he laid the flat of his hand there, she swallowed a gasp of pleasure at the feel of his palm on her belly.

He fanned out the tips of his fingers to draw his nails lightly across the quivering surface of her skin. His thumb brushed the darker blonde curls. She lay motionless, holding her breath, resisting a wanton urge to arch her hips and open her tingling thighs.

'I have too many clothes on.' Wolfe lifted her legs from his lap and, rising, placed them on the bed. Still caressing her body with his eyes, he began to undress, quickly shrugging out of his coat and dragging his shirt free from his pants with an urgency that sent new tremors through her.

Soon he was as naked as she, his powerful wide-shouldered physique outlined against the window as he said, 'Move over, *ma belle*.'

Suzy wriggled herself from the edge to the centre of the bed. With lithe ease, he lay down beside her and took her in his arms, taking care not to crush her breasts against the hard wall of his chest.

She slipped her arms round his neck, still scarcely able to believe this wasn't a dream, she was really in bed with him, able to feel his heart beating close to her own, to inhale the clean smell of his skin, to stroke the back of his head as she had so often longed to, and to feel, between their clasped bodies, the proof of his impatience to take her.

But it wasn't until much later, after more than once making her cry out in protest as he forced her over the edge of control into a vortex of ecstasy that, at last, he unleashed his own need.

As his body invaded hers, in an act of triumphant conquest to which she willingly surrendered, she felt a brief tearing pain. It lasted only a second or two. Then their bodies fused in the ultimate closeness. Almost at once the fleeting agony was forgotten. With a primeval thrill, she felt the strong rhythmic thrusts, slow at first and then faster and faster until, with one last wild plunge, it was over, except for the gradual quietening of their breathing, and the wonderful sense of total relaxation, total peace.

For a long time neither of them moved. She would have liked to stroke his back and brush little loving kisses along the top of his shoulder which was only inches from her mouth. But she kept her hands still and her head on the pillow, grateful that at least he was staying with her, not withdrawing and moving away in the classic post-coitus put-down. That would have been unbearable.

That he fell asleep in her arms was another matter. Even though, with the weight of his chest no longer supported by his arms, he soon became uncomfortably heavy, she didn't mind.

She knew she had done the right thing. Whatever happened tomorrow, she would have this wonderful night to remember for the rest of her life. Every kiss, every touch had confirmed her belief that Wolfe would be a skilful and considerate lover.

As she lay motionless under his long, lax form, looking into the future, wondering how—when the time came—she would find the strength to go away, Wolfe began to wake up.

Almost at once he realised he had been crushing her and raised himself on his elbows.

'I'm sorry. Why didn't you wake me?'

He bent his head to brush several light, tender kisses on her temples and cheeks.

Her answer was to hug him to her; suppressing a longing to whisper softly, 'I love you.'

After a moment or two, he moved from between her spread thighs to stretch his long limbs on the mattress. Turning to face the windows, he turned Suzy with him, arranging her comfortably in his arms with her back to his chest and one arm encircling her body.

She felt a last kiss on her shoulder. For a second or two he fondled the breast he was holding. Then his fingers stilled and she knew he had gone back to sleep—leaving her with the uneasy feeling that, between waking and going to sleep again, he had thought she was one of his other women.

CHAPTER EIGHT

Suzy wakened slowly, knowing before she opened her eyes that she had slept long and deeply.

As was usual when she awoke, she was lying on her side with her knees drawn up. Slowly, she straightened her legs, stretching herself like a cat.

It was the sudden realisation that she was naked which made her open her eyes, expecting to see Wolfe beside her. But he wasn't there. She had the huge bed to herself.

The memory of all the heavenly things he had done to her, and how, with their bodies still fused, he had fallen asleep in her arms, made her give a long sigh of pleasure.

It had been the most wonderful experience of her life, infinitely worth waiting for. It had made her feel a new person; as if those blissful tremors, shudders and convulsions had rearranged all her cells and left her with this lovely feeling of mental and physical wellbeing. Head-to-toe, total wellbeing.

After a minute or two, she rolled on to her back and sat up, pulling three of the pillows into a heap and settling herself against them. From force of habit she drew the sheet up to cover herself.

Presumably Wolfe was in the bathroom, shaving and having a shower. When he came back, would he make love to her again? She hoped so. It was Sunday. They could spend the whole day in bed if they chose.

The inner door opened. Wolfe re-entered his bedroom. He was wearing a white towelling robe. His brown feet were bare and his hair was damp.

'Good morning,' he said, coming towards her. He wasn't smiling. She couldn't tell what his mood was.

'Good morning.' The smile she gave him was radiant.

Why should she hide that—thanks to him—she felt terrific?

He sat down on the end of the bed and looked thoughtfully at her.

'How long have you been awake?'

'About five minutes. Have you been up long?'

'Half an hour. How are you feeling this morning?'

'Marvellous.'

'No headache?'

'Why should I have a headache?' she asked blankly.

'You had rather a lot to drink last night.'

'Did I? I didn't realise I had more than anyone else.'

'Possibly not, but perhaps you had more than you usually drink—enough to undermine your judgment. But I have a harder head, there's no excuse for my behaviour.' He frowned. 'I wanted you and I took you.'

'With my full co-operation,' Suzy said, with a nervous laugh.

His reaction confused her. That he would regret last night was the last thing she had expected.

'Oh, Wolfe, please don't look so grim! Nothing bad has happened,' she exclaimed. 'If I don't regret it, why should you?'

His dark eyes narrowed. 'Don't you regret it?'

'Not a bit. It was wonderful. But I do wish you'd kiss me good morning instead of sitting over there.' She sat up and held out her arms.

The sheet fell away from her breasts. She saw him look at them. A moment later she was in his arms, and his mouth was inches from hers.

'But you will regret it, I'm afraid. We both shall. Mixing business and pleasure never works,' he said, before he kissed her.

The cool, fresh taste of his mouth made her want to brush her own teeth.

After a moment or two she pushed him away. 'Let me have five minutes in the bathroom, then I'll be right back. Do you keep a spare toothbrush in there?'

'In the right-hand cupboard.'

As she freed herself from his embrace and from the bedclothes, his hands slid over the smooth, warm curves of her body, making her impatient to return to him.

She was halfway across the room when she heard him say sharply, 'My God!'

She turned.

Wolfe was staring at the centre of the bed. 'There's blood on the sheet!' He looked at her, his tanned face taut with concern. 'I must have hurt you like hell. Why didn't you tell me?'

'You didn't . . . or only for a moment.' Dismayed that so slight an injury should have left such a large, tell-tale stain on the snowy perçale, she murmured, 'Oh dear! What on earth will the maid think?'

'Let her think what she likes,' he said abruptly. 'It's you I'm worried about. We must get a doctor to look at you. Even if you haven't done this for a long time, it isn't normal to bleed.' He strode to where she was standing and put his arms round her. 'My poor girl! What can I say? Why didn't you stop me, for God's sake?'

Suzy buried her face against his shoulder. This was a complication she hadn't foreseen. She had thought that visible evidence of virginity was a relic of Victorian wedding nights when ignorant brides submitted, rigid with terror, to being quickly and clumsily 'deflowered'.

'I didn't want you to stop. It was wonderful,' she told him, in a muffled voice.

He stroked her hair. 'But you've just admitted that I hurt you.'

'Only for a fraction of a second. The rest was bliss—truly it was.' She parted the front of his robe and pressed a soft, loving kiss against his hard, sunbrowned chest. 'But I'm horribly embarrassed about the sheet. It's bound to cause gossip among the maids.'

Wolfe put her gently away from him.

'The maids can gossip their heads off. Forget it. Go and brush your teeth while I make some coffee.'

'Could I borrow something to wear? One of your dressing gowns?'

He nodded and went to a closet from which he produced a cotton happi coat of the kind issued to passengers on Oriental airlines.

'This will fit you better than a dressing gown.'

His bathroom was as large as her bedroom, with a shower, a sunken tub and a handbasin set in a counter of dark polished marble. Apart from a space on the hot rails where a towel was missing—and was now, presumably, in a concealed laundry container—there was little to show the bathroom had already been used. Clearly, in spite of his luxurious lifestyle, his personal habits were disciplined and orderly.

When Suzy returned to the bedroom, he was drinking coffee by the window. He rose from his chair as she entered, and didn't sit down until she had taken the other chair.

'I was going to order breakfast, but on second thoughts it will be better for us to have it separately,' he said, pouring coffee for her. 'There's a slight chance someone will see you going back to your room. But if you have breakfast here in that thing, or your evening clothes, it will be tantamount to announcing that we've spent the night together. For the sake of your reputation, I think we should be as discreet as possible.'

She sipped the hot fragrant coffee he had made in the butler's pantry. She said, 'And you always run before breakfast, even on Sundays.'

'Not always. Certainly not today. As soon as we've eaten, I'll take you to a gynaecologist. That lesion may need some treatment.'

'It's nothing, Wolfe . . . really nothing. Please don't worry about it . . . and I certainly don't need to see a doctor, especially on a Sunday morning.'

'You'll do as you're told,' he said firmly. 'I know an excellent consultant who gave Hannah a check when she thought she might have a problem. He won't mind seeing you today when I explain the circumstances.'

'But you can't! I mean . . . what will he think?'

'What people will think seems to bother you more than your health.'

'There's nothing wrong with my health. You're making a fuss about nothing.' Suzy strove to keep her voice level. 'Please let it drop. I assure you I'm perfectly all right.'

Wolfe gave her a searching look before he said, 'I think you know there's something wrong and you're afraid to find out what it is. That's a crazy attitude, Susan. Probably it's some minor condition which can very easily be corrected. Tell me something: is it possible that you haven't been to bed with anyone since your husband died?'

Avoiding his gaze, she said, 'No . . . no, I haven't.'

'And that was how long ago? Four years?'

She nodded.

'Then more than likely that explains it. I should have been more gentle with you.'

'You were.'

'Not gentle enough for someone who's lived like a nun for four years. That's a long time in this day and age—especially for someone with your temperament. I thought the first time I saw you that your mouth didn't match your manner.'

He leaned across the low table and touched her lips

with his forefinger. For the first time a glimmer of amusement came into his eyes.

'That wasn't a one-night stand, was it? You want us to make love again?'

Her lip quivered under his touch. 'Very much,' she agreed, in a low tone.

'Then be a good girl and stop fussing. There's no need to feel embarrassed. A consultant who, so I've heard, is confessor to some of the most promiscuous women in New York isn't likely to raise his eyebrows——'

He stopped short, his own brows contracting. 'If you haven't had sex for four years, does that mean you're not on the pill?'

'No, I'm not,' she admitted.

With a groan of exasperation, he sank back in his chair and pressed the tips of his fingers against his closed eyelids.

Suzy could tell he was furious with her. But it was a question she had never expected him to ask and it had taken her by surprise. Instinctively honest, never able to lie convincingly, she had blurted out the truth.

Wolfe lowered his hands and looked at her, shaking his head in a gesture of baffled disbelief that anyone could be so feckless.

'Why, in God's name, didn't you tell me?'

'I . . . I don't know.'

It was all going hideously wrong; her plan which had seemed so foolproof the night before.

Wolfe reached for the coffee pot and refilled his cup. His anger seemed to have abated, or at least was under control now. He even said, 'More for you?' to her.

'I haven't finished this yet.'

He picked up his cup and saucer and carried it across the room to his bed. There he put them down on the night table, sat on the edge of the bed and

opened a cupboard fitted with spaces for eight or nine
telephone directories; European ones as well as those
for Manhattan.

As he looked for the number he wanted, he said,
'Whoever said "Never explain, never apologise"
should have added "Never assume". Even the
reasonable assumption that no intelligent woman in
her middle twenties would chance getting pregnant
can be mistaken, it seems.'

The quiet but scalpel-sharp sarcasm made her
flinch. She wondered what he would say if she told
him she wanted his child.

'This time we may have been lucky, but I shouldn't
like to count on it.' He reached for the telephone.

Suzy knew then that she had to tell him the whole
truth. There was no way out of it.

'No, stop . . . wait a minute . . . please, Wolfe,' she
exclaimed, as he started to tap out the number.

Her tone was sufficiently urgent to make him stop
dialling.

'You're not going to tell me you don't approve
of——'

'No, it isn't that,' she cut in quickly. 'I will go to the
doctor about that—but not today. If I went today it
would only make us both look foolish. You . . . you
asked me how long it was since I last made love. I—
I've never made love before. Until last night I was a
virgin.'

It was the first time she had ever seen Wolfe
disconcerted. After staring at her for some moments,
he replaced the receiver on its rest.

'I thought you were married for some time before
your husband died?'

'A year and a half.'

She bowed her head, twisting the circle of gold on
her left hand, remembering the day Chris had slipped
it over her finger.

Wolfe rose from the bed and came back to the chair near hers.

'I think you'd better tell me everything.'

Suzy lifted her chin and fixed her gaze on a lamp on the far side of the room.

'We were going to spend our honeymoon in Scotland, partly in Edinburgh and partly touring the west coast. We were married at eleven in the morning and we left the reception at three, intending to spend our wedding night at Dryburgh Abbey, about forty miles south of Edinburgh.'

She paused, her mouth suddenly dry.

'We never got there. We spent the night in hospital at Newcastle. A car in the slow lane had a blow-out and swerved across the fast lane. If that lane had happened to be clear, nothing very much might have happened. But it wasn't. There were three cars in the fast lane. Four people died and seven were seriously injured. One of them was Chris . . . my husband.'

Wolfe said nothing, waiting for her to continue.

'I was hardly hurt at all,' she went on. 'They discharged me in less than a week. But I couldn't go home because Chris was still desperately ill. He . . . he almost died, but somehow they pulled him through.' Her lips trembled for a moment. 'Later . . . I wished they hadn't,' she said, with a break in her voice.

In case he should misunderstand, she turned to him, eyes bright with tears.

'Not for myself . . . never for a moment for myself. For him. Poor darling Chris.'

The tears spilled over and coursed slowly down her cheeks.

'You see . . . he'd lost both legs, and not only that . . . he had other terrible injuries.'

As she tried to wipe away the tears with the back of her hand, to her horror she broke down completely. The buried anguish of the past rose up in a wild gush

of feeling which she had no power to control. Fresh
tears brimmed over her eyelids and she found herself
starting to sob.

Wolfe rose from his chair. Before she knew what he
was doing, he had lifted her on to his lap.

As she lay across his long thighs, her head against
his broad shoulder, it was like being a child again; a
little girl safely enfolded in the strong, loving arms of
her father.

As, gradually, her grief subsided, he produced from
the pocket of his robe a large clean linen handkerchief.
Suzy mopped her wet cheeks and blew her nose.

'I'm sorry,' she murmured huskily.

He was silent. Without sitting up, she couldn't see
his expression. Reluctant to move as long as he let her
remain there, she gave a long unsteady sigh and stayed
where she was, the storm spent.

After a while he said quietly, 'You never lived
together before you were married?'

'Oh, no—people don't in north Yorkshire. At least
not as often as in London. I was living at home with
my family. So was he. Our parents would have had a
fit if we'd moved out and set up home together,
without being married. They know it happens in other
places, but not in a small town like ours. People still
get engaged there. Chris and I were engaged for six
months.'

'And you never made love in that time? Why not?
Most people do.'

'I know, and Chris wanted us to, but I didn't.
Afterwards I wished I had. It was my greatest regret.'

'Why didn't you want to?'

'Oh ... there were all kinds of difficulties. I
couldn't face seeing our doctor, an old man who
wouldn't have approved. Also there was nowhere to go
... nowhere to be really private. In summer it might
have been different, but it was winter—a bad one. To

make love in the car seemed ... sordid. I was very young for my age, and rather inhibited, I suppose. I wanted to wait for the honeymoon when there wouldn't be anything to worry about. I think, at that time, I was more interested in the wedding arrangements, and in furnishing the cottage Chris's parents had given us, than in marriage itself. It was only after we were married that I realised what we had lost ... that I finally grew up.'

When he didn't say anything, she went on, 'That was why, last night, when I could have backed out, I didn't. A long time ago I made up my mind that, next time, if someone wanted me, and I wanted him ...' She left the rest unexpressed.

'Are you sure it was me you wanted, or merely to end an over-long virginity?'

His caustic tone startled and hurt her. She straightened and rose from his lap.

Going back to the chair she had left, she said stiffly, 'If that had been a problem, the world is full of men who would have helped me to solve it. I wanted my first experience to be with someone I ... respected.'

Wolfe sprang up from his chair and began to pace restlessly across the room, his clenched fists thrust deep inside the pockets of his terry robe.

'Knowing damn well that, if I'd guessed you were a virgin, I wouldn't have touched you,' he said angrily.

'Why not? What difference does it make?'

'Years ago I made it a rule never to become involved with women who weren't fully mature, independent, rational beings. Young girls, however attractive, have always been strictly off limits.'

'I'm not a young girl.'

'Not in years, but you have no experience—or hadn't, until I seduced you,' he added, with a snap.

'That's absurd! You didn't seduce me. I spent the whole of last evening making it clear that I ... I was

available. I wanted it to happen, and I don't regret it
now it has. From everything one hears, the first time
is usually a horrible disappointment. It wasn't like
that in my case. You made it wonderful for me.'

Afterwards it struck her that most men would have
been mollified by such a tribute. Not Wolfe.

He said brusquely, 'Any man who couldn't give
pleasure to a partner as responsive as you are would
have to be a blundering idiot. I may not be that kind
of fool, but obviously I'm slipping in other ways. God!
I should have my head examined. I knew last night
there was a risk of fouling up our working
relationship, but it didn't even cross my mind I was
going to bed with a girl who was trusting to luck there
would be no worse repercussions. Did you think I
shouldn't like it if you asked me to make sure there
were none? Or did you just cross your fingers and
hope for the best?'

She flinched from the last of his sarcascm.

'If ... if anything happens, it will be *my*
responsibility. I shan't blame you, or ask you to help
me. I shall ... handle it myself,' she said stiffly.

Inwardly, she wanted to weep. It was all turning out
so differently from the way she had envisaged.

'Oh, you will, will you?' Wolfe rasped furiously. He
strode back to where she was sitting and thrust a hard
hand under her chin, turning her face up to his. 'If that
means what I think—forget it. You're not the type to
take that solution in your stride. It would leave nasty
scars on your psyche. Besides which, I don't propose to
be kept in the dark a second time. If you do get pregnant,
we'll decide what to do about it together.'

He released his hold on her chin. 'Now go and have
a hot bath while I dress and go down to your room.
What clothes do you want me to bring you?'

With an effort Suzy collected her wits and told him
where to find some suitable clothes.

'The box my dress was packed in is on the bed. You could put them in that,' she suggested.

Presently, lying up to her neck in warm water, she wondered if, now, because he had found out about her, he wouldn't make love to her again. Her heart sank at the thought of never repeating an experience which had been all and more than she had anticipated.

She wondered what he had meant by saying that anyone who couldn't give pleasure to a partner as responsive as herself would have to be a blundering idiot.

Did that mean she was more responsive than the other women in his life? She didn't see how she could have been. Unless the fact that she loved him made some subtle difference. But she had always suspected that Lady Belinda loved him, even if Jacqueline Dupont didn't.

She was still stretched out in the bath when there was a knock on the door and she heard him ask, 'May I come in?'

She sat up quickly. 'Of course.'

Wolfe walked in and put the dress box on the bench in front of the dressing counter. Then he looked at her.

'You keep your room very tidy. A place for everything and everything in its place.'

'I try to be reasonably organised.'

He pulled one of the thick fluffy bath sheets from the bank of heated chrome rails and shook out its folds.

'Out you get.'

She stood up, her wet skin glistening, drops of water beading her shoulders and thighs. In the absence of a bath cap, she had used one of the linen hand towels as an improvised turban to keep her hair off her neck.

She felt Wolfe's eyes appraising her as she stepped

over the rim of the bath on to the mat. Then he wrapped the towel round her.

The last time someone had enveloped her in a warm towel she had been a child, flat-chested and hipless. Now she was intensely aware of being, at long last, a woman; a different being from the Suzy Walker of yesterday.

She expected him to leave her to dry herself and get dressed. Instead he stayed, his hands moving over her body, briskly at first and then more and more slowly and caressingly until, very soon, she was longing for him to take the towel away and stroke her bare flesh.

She could tell by the way he was watching her that he was doing it deliberately and waiting to see her reaction. At first she tried not to show any; to stand still, her expression impassive. Soon that became impossible. She began to feel weak at the knees and to need to make sinuous movements in response to the pressure of his hands.

Just as it was impossible not to snuggle deeper into one's coat when stepping outside the hotel on a biting day in winter, it wasn't possible to feel his palms moulding the curves of her hips and buttocks without wanting to give a sensuous squirm of delight. Nor could she go on breathing normally. Her lungs seemed to need more and more air. She found herself breathing through parted lips, panting almost.

Wolfe himself appeared to be unmoved. Suzy could see no sign that her mounting excitement was mutual.

'Please . . .' she murmured helplessly. 'Don't . . .'

'Don't?' His raised eyebrow mocked her.

Then abruptly his head swooped down, catching her mouth in a kiss which quickly revealed that his air of detachment had been misleading.

She felt him pull off the turban, releasing her hair. Moments later the bath sheet began to slide from her shoulders, held from falling below her waist by the pressure of the arm which was clasping her to him while his free hand tilted her head back.

Suzy clung to him, dizzy with pleasure and relief that it wasn't only she who had wanted this. Responding with passionate abandonment to the fierce demand of his kisses and roving hands, she forgot that a short time ago he had seemed to be angry with her. All that mattered was that now he wasn't: how he was straining her to him in a kiss which she knew was the prelude to total possession of her eager-to-be-ravished senses.

He took her right there, in the bathroom, on the dense cream pile of the carpet, with more towels flung down to cushion her shoulders and hips. Her recent immersion in the bath seemed to have made her skin more sensitive. Every movement of his hands, every exploration by his lips made her writhe with exquisite sensations. Even the beams of brilliance from the downlighters in the bathroom ceiling couldn't inhibit her response. There was no way she could hide the completeness of her surrender.

Afterwards Wolfe didn't stay with her long. Leaving her sprawled on the floor, her heartbeat gradually resuming its normal rhythm, he rose to his feet and disappeared into the shower.

For some minutes she stayed where she was, listening to the sound of the water, feeling too languorous to move.

She wondered what the people who knew her, or thought they did—her parents and sisters, Hannah and Alix, the friends she had made at her exercise classes—would think if they could see her now.

Would they be shocked? Would they think she was out of her mind?

They might. She didn't. She could never remember feeling more truly alive; more truly herself.

Presently she picked herself up and stepped back

into the bath to refresh her hot, dewy skin. It was only then that it struck her as strange and puzzling that Wolfe, having taken her to task for behaving irresponsibly, should almost immediately afterwards initiate a repetition of her recklessness.

He was taking a long time in the shower, considering that he had already had one. She wished she knew what he was thinking as he stood under the cascading water, the outlines of his tall form blurred by the bubbly design on the sliding glass panels.

She was dry and wearing her underclothes before he emerged, a towel wrapped round his lean hips. Poised on one leg, the other foot in her pantyhose, Suzy paused to smile at him.

'What would you like for breakfast?' he asked.

Suzy remembered the first time he had asked her that question. Unsure of herself and nervous of him, she had chosen the first thing which came into her head. This time she deliberated for as long as it took to finish rolling up her tights.

'Prunes . . . yoghurt . . . liver and bacon with grilled tomatoes . . . wholemeal toast with honey and tea, please.'

He nodded. She saw him taking in her underpinnings; the white satin and lace bra and the matching panties he had taken from her underwear drawer, and the sheer black tights she liked to wear with the black pleated skirt and black and white herringbone top she had asked him to bring from her closet.

Since taking Hannah's advice about her clothes, she had stopped having up to a dozen sets of inexpensive chain-store lingerie. Now she never had more than three sets of really exquisite French undies and although, until today, no one other than saleswomen had seen the pretty wisps she wore under her suits and dresses, it had made her feel good to be well dressed right down to her skin.

Now, with Wolfe's eyes upon her, she was even more glad she had changed to more seductive underclothes. Perhaps from now on she should make another change—to stockings. Men were supposed to find them sexier than pantyhose, and if she wanted to hold his interest she would have to use every wile in the book.

At this moment, however, he seemed to find black tights alluring. He came to where she was standing and slid his hands over her hips, looking down at the cleavage displayed by the delicate lace.

'You have an unexpected talent for making me feel like a twenty-year-old stud,' he said, pulling her against him. 'I'm tempted to——' He broke off, smiling and shaking his head. 'No, I think not. After breakfast, perhaps.'

Dropping a kiss on her forehead, he drew back and turned away, leaving her to finish dressing.

Before she joined him for breakfast, she spent a few minutes in her office so that if the breakfast waiter was still in the living-room he would think she had started work early. That she should work on a Sunday wouldn't surprise him; her employer's idiosyncratic habits were well-known.

However, the man had already gone when she entered the living-room, and Wolfe was seated at the table, but was waiting for her to join him before he began his breakfast.

He rose and drew out the other chair for her.

'Very discreet,' was his comment, as she crossed the wide room towards him. 'Will it worry you if people find out we're sleeping together?'

'I would rather not advertise the fact,' she admitted. 'Not so much on my own account, but for my parents' sake. I know it would upset them. They hold rather old-fashioned views.'

'In that case perhaps we should regularise our relationship,' he said, as he seated himself.

In the act of unfolding her napkin, Suzy froze. 'How do you mean?'

The telephone started to ring. Wolfe said, 'I'll get it,' and rose again. As he walked away from the table, he added, speaking over his shoulder, 'Perhaps we should get married.'

CHAPTER NINE

THROUGHOUT his short conversation with whoever was calling—afterwards Suzy had no recollection of a single word of his side of it—she stared at the back of his head, unable to believe she could possibly have heard him aright.

Wolfe replaced the receiver and returned.

'Well ... what do you think?' he enquired, re-seating himself.

'I—I think you must be joking,' she said faintly.

He picked up the spoon for his fruit but paused before starting to eat.

'I don't want my children's friends to mistake me for their grandfather,' he answered. 'And if you also want children, it's better to have them before you're thirty.'

He *was* serious! she thought incredulously.

'But ... why me? Why not——?' She left the question unfinished. He must know what she was thinking.

'Because I believe we shall suit each other. We've already established that we can work together on a day-to-day basis without getting on each other's nerves.'

'You established that with Hannah.'

'True, but Hannah didn't attract me sexually.'

'I didn't think I did—until last night.'

'Oh, yes—very much so,' he told her. 'But it didn't seem a good idea to do anything about it. Last night was one of the very rare occasions in my life when I've ignored what I thought was my better judgment.' He smiled at her. 'Maybe I should do it more often.'

After a pause, Suzy said, 'The very first day I started working for you, I annoyed you by making a remark about your . . . private life. At the risk of making you angry, there's something I have to ask you.'

'The circumstances are different now. Go ahead, ask whatever you like.'

'Everyone knows you used to have three and still have two close friendships. Why have you never asked Lady Belinda or Madame Dupont to marry you?'

Without hesitation, he answered, 'Because their companionship is like caviar. I enjoy it, but I don't want it every day. For marriage one has to find a woman who is like bread and cheese and apples. Those are things which one can eat daily without getting tired of them. Caviar—even fresh Royal Beluga—palls if one has too much of it. Aren't you going to eat your prunes?'

Suzy realised that all she had done so far was to push them round the dish. 'Oh . . . yes.' She began to eat, but without her usual enjoyment of the dark fruit topped with creamy yoghurt.

'But surely you wouldn't want never to have caviar again?' she ventured presently.

Wolfe looked up, his eyes enigmatic as they met hers across the table.

'Certainly not—in the literal sense. Figuratively—it depends. On my wife. Few men look elsewhere for pleasures they can find at home,' he said dryly.

There was another silence until she said, 'What about love?'

'Love, in my observation, is the culmination of a marriage, not its starting point. Most young people marry or begin living together on a basis of sexual attraction. They don't find out if they like each other until later. I consider a couple can be said to love each other when they've been together for twenty years and still have good sex and plenty to talk about.'

'You're very . . . down to earth.'

'That shouldn't come as any surprise. By now you should be familiar with all my peculiarities. *Il n'y a pas de héros pour son valet de chambre . . . ou son secrétaire.*'

No man is a hero to his valet . . . or his secretary.

She thought: Unless she happens to be in love with him. Love transforms all men into gods.

Aloud, she said, 'I still can't believe you're serious.'

'I've been thinking about marriage for some time. It's always been in my mind to have a large family—when I could find a suitable partner. Until this morning, I didn't realise that an eminently suitable candidate was right in front of me. Once you get used to the idea, you'll see what good sense it makes. You do want to have children, don't you?'

'Yes—yes, very much. When you say "a large family", how many——'

'At least four. Possibly more.'

'Supposing you married me and we didn't have any. What then?'

'An unlikely eventuality. We'll worry about that when it happens.'

Was he being diplomatic? Not saying that, if she failed to produce the heirs he wanted, he would divorce her and look for someone who could. The possibility chilled her.

She had sometimes dreamed of being his wife; an impossible dream she had known could never be realised. Yet now that it was within her grasp, she hesitated to seize the opportunity. She knew why. Always in her fantasies, he had been in love with her. Her daydreams had never included this prosaic kind of proposal.

'I'll have to think about it,' she said. 'I can't make important decisions as quickly as you do.'

'By all means, but don't spend too long thinking.

When I make a decision I like to act on it. You should
be able to make up your mind by tonight.'

'By tonight!' she exclaimed, in consternation. 'But
that's much too soon. I shall need much more than
one day.'

'Nonsense. The longer you think it over, the less
sure you'll become,' Wolfe said bracingly.

Two weeks later, with her first wedding ring
replaced by another, Suzy found herself on Pan
Am's non-stop flight to Munich, bound for a
honeymoon the exact location of which Wolfe had
not yet revealed to her.

It was dark when they landed in Germany. It didn't
surprise her to find a luxurious limousine awaiting
them, but that it was an English Rolls-Royce was
unexpected.

'I'm afraid we still have some way to go. About an
hour's run,' Wolfe told her. 'But I think you'll find
when we get there that the journey has been
worthwhile.'

For the first time it occurred to her to wonder if, on
his previous visit or visits to the place he had chosen,
he had been with a party of people—perhaps on a
skiing holiday—or with a woman.

Surely he wouldn't bring his wife to a place where
he had stayed with one of his mistresses?

His wife. Even though she was wearing his ring, and
already a number of people had addressed her as Mrs
Vyner, she found it hard to believe they were married.
The brief ceremony which had taken place first thing
that morning had been as simple as her first wedding
had been elaborate.

She had worn the wheat-coloured sweater, baby-
buttoned on the left shoulder, and matching skirt by
St John in which she was travelling. The weather
being mild, she hadn't needed a coat. However, on the

way to the airport Wolfe had produced a fur which he
said she might need in Europe. It was a hip-length
jacket of natural Canadian lynx, enormously chic
and—she guessed—enormously expensive. It was his
second lavish gift. He had insisted she keep the
Bulgari necklace and ear-rings.

She had not worn the coat on the plane. A
stewardess had taken it away and brought it back when
they landed. Now, sitting in the back of the car with a
rug tucked round her knees and the upper part of her
body enveloped in the opulent fur, she couldn't resist
stroking its fluffy, silky texture. It was a wonderful
colour, blending beige and silver with darker markings;
the kind of fur which went with country tweeds or
sophisticated city clothes.

From the airport, on the outskirts of Munich, they
did not have to pass through the city to reach
wherever they were going. There being no moon,
there wasn't much to be seen.

Suzy wished Wolfe would put his arm round her, or
at least hold her hand. So far his manner towards her
had been little different than on their previous
journeys together—courteous, considerate but in no
way romantic.

Indeed, since the morning he had asked her to
marry him, he had not made love to her again. She
had slept in her room, as before. Having forced her to
make up her mind in the space of a day, he had given
her a week to change it. But when, at the end of the
week, she had reaffirmed her decision—expecting to
be whisked into bed—he had said that he thought it
best if they continued to behave circumspectly until
they were married.

By then she had been longing to spend another
night in his arms and had been both puzzled and
disturbed by his lack of ardour. In the week leading up
to their wedding, Wolfe had kissed her cheek or her

hand more often than her mouth. His restraint had been almost Victorian.

Presently a glimpse of a signpost made her turn to him, asking, 'Are we going to Salzburg?'

'No, but we'll be spending some of our time there.'

'I'd forgotten that Munich is close to the border with Austria. I've always wanted to see Salzburg. Have you been to the Festival?'

She knew that in late July and August the city became a mecca for music lovers from all over the world.

'Yes—twice. Next year, if you like, we can go together. But Salzburg has a lot to recommend it apart from the Festival. We're going to stay in what's called the Salzkammergut, Austria's lake district. But that's all I'm going to tell you.'

To her delight, he reached for her hand and squeezed it gently in his larger, stronger hand. Suzy gave an answering squeeze and then, on impulse, she lifted the hand and pressed her parted lips softly against the back of his palm.

When, a few moments later, he removed his hand from around hers, she wondered if her gesture might have been too demonstrative. Maybe he liked to set the pace and she would be wise not to volunteer caresses.

But even as this thought occurred to her, he slipped his hand under the rug, found the hem of her skirt and slid his warm palm up her leg, his fingers stroking the inside of her thigh.

She was wearing sheer stockings with a garter belt. When his fingertips touched her bare skin, she felt a spasm of pleasure so sharp that her whole body jerked and she only just managed to stifle an audible gasp.

It was frightening how easily Wolfe could make her lose control. She sat with closed eyes, cocooned in the luxurious fur, trembling at the intimate caress of his fingertips between the top of her stocking and the lacy edge of her panties.

At last, when every nerve in her body seemed to be pulsating with excitement, he stopped the incredibly sensual feather-soft massage, put her skirt back in place and withdrew his hand.

For her, the rest of the journey passed in a haze of longing for the moment when they would be alone together. It shouldn't be long after their arrival at wherever they were staying. Had they crossed the Atlantic in the other direction, they would have arrived with hours to wait before bedtime, by which time she, if not he, would have been needing sleep rather than love.

This way, travelling east to west, it was already mid-evening in Austria. No one would look askance if after a long flight they chose to retire early—even though by their body-clocks it was still only afternoon.

Less than two hours after their arrival at Munich, Suzy found herself sitting by a blazing log fire in their private sitting-room, sipping the champagne which Wolfe had poured for her before going to have his shower.

She had already bathed; a bath run for her by the maid who had unpacked her cases and laid out her night things. She was wearing them now, a long robe of couleur-de-rose panne velvet, with satin facings and bindings, over a bias-cut 1930s-style nightgown of shell pink slipper satin. Her trousseau slippers were high-heeled quilted silk mules trimmed with ostrich feather puffs—the kind of slippers her grandmothers might have worn on their honeymoons had they been the daughters of rich men.

She wondered how her family would react when, tomorrow or the day after, they received the letter telling them that by the time it reached them she would be married to Wolfe.

She had felt it best to write rather than telephone. It was easier to break the news gently in a long, carefully-phrased letter than in a long-distance conversation. It was bound to come as a shock to them. She had seldom mentioned Wolfe in her letters.

A painful shock, probably. She had an uneasy feeling they would take offence because Wolfe hadn't presented himself to them before marrying her. In Yorkshire, among people like her parents, it wasn't done to marry in haste with none of one's family or friends present. A widow was allowed to marry quietly, but not in a rushed, hole-and-corner way, which was how they would regard the brief civil ceremony which had given them a new son-in-law, one they had never set eyes on.

However, thinking about it, she knew that she didn't really care what her family thought. From now on Wolfe was the only important person in her life.

She remembered a phrase spoken by the clergyman who had conducted her first wedding. *Forsaking all other, keep thee only unto him . . .*

And a verse from an Arab love poem read a long time ago and perhaps not remembered accurately. How had it gone?

Leave thy father and thy mother,
Leave thy brothers and thy sisters.
What need'st thou thy tribe's black tents
Who hast the red pavilion of my heart?

She sighed. Wolfe had not offered her his heart; only his luxurious lifestyle, his skill as a lover, and the chance to be the mother of his children. Which was more, far more, than she had hoped for on the night she had given herself to him.

She knew she ought to be glad to be his wife on any terms. No one ever had everything in life, and for what she would have from now on many women would gladly change places with her.

Taking another sip of champagne, she looked round the beautiful room with its heavy interlined silk curtains, antique furniture, paintings and flowers.

'This is more like a private house than a hotel. What is it called?' she asked, as her husband strolled through from the bedroom, wearing a dark brown silk robe and black leather slippers.

'Schloss Fuschl. Austria has a number of castles which have been turned into hotels, and this is one of the best of them. It dates from the fifteenth and sixteenth centuries. As you'll see tomorrow, some of the public rooms are very fine.'

Wolfe poured some champagne for himself, replenished her glass and sat down beside her on the feather-cushioned sofa upholstered with pale beige silk tweed.

As he stretched out his long, suntanned legs, lightly furred with dark hair, she realised he wasn't wearing pyjamas, only the heavy silk robe.

'To us,' he said, raising his glass.

'To us,' she echoed.

They drank, watching each other.

'Has it seemed long since the last time you spent the night with me?' he asked her.

'Yes,' she admitted, after a brief hesitation.

He smiled, but he didn't tell her it had seemed a long time to him.

'Why don't you take off that dressing-gown? I'm sure you aren't cold,' he suggested.

After another hesitation Suzy put down her glass and stood up. The robe had a satin-lined sash, held at the sides by silk loops. She untied it and let the ends fall. Then she drew the robe off her shoulders, feeling the sleeves slide down her arms, curling her fingers to catch them, fold the soft, supple velvet and throw it lightly across one of the two large armchairs which faced the sofa from the opposite side of the chimneybreast.

Then she stood on the deep white fur rug in her satin nightdress, watching his slow appraisal of the clinging cut of the lustrous fabric. Just by looking at her like that he could make her breasts swell, her belly flutter with excitement.

Her throat tight, she watched him drain his glass, at the same time reaching a long arm to switch off the lamp on the end table. He rose and moved about the room, turning out all the other lights until only the leaping roseate glow of the flames remained.

As he came back to where she was standing, he said, 'I like your nightgown, but I don't think you're going to need it except in the unlikely event of a fire alarm. I always sleep in the raw—as you will from now on.'

A few feet away, he stopped, his hands thrust into the pockets of his robe. She knew he was waiting for her to shed her nightie, and wouldn't move until she did.

Slowly she lifted her hands and pushed first one strap and then the other over the ends of her shoulders. The nightgown wasn't loose enough to slip down her body of its own volition. She had to pull it down to her waist and then ease it over her hips until, at the top of her thighs, it fell in a pool round her feet. She stepped over it, stooped, picked it up and tossed it on top of her robe.

When she turned to face Wolfe again, he had flung off his own dressing-gown and was as naked as she, his tall, wide-shouldered frame bronzed by the flickering firelight.

Their arms hanging loosely at their sides, they faced each other, the soft crackling of the burning logs the only sound in the shadowy room.

Without lowering her gaze from his face, Suzy knew his whole body was taut with urgent desire. Perhaps it was a trick of the light, but his eyes seemed to gleam with a passion which made her a little afraid of the fierce male animal power no longer leashed and controlled by his urbane public persona.

For a moment or two she felt like a small helpless creature about to be savaged by a predator. He was so much taller and stronger; his whole body armoured with muscle, equipped to drive deep into hers whether she wished it or not.

In that moment, as he moved towards her, her instinct was to recoil. But she didn't. She stayed very still, scarcely breathing as, taking her wrists, he raised her arms until her hands were at the back of his neck. Leaving them there, he lowered his hands to her waist and moved closer until the tips of her breasts were brushing his chest and lower down she could feel a heated but unexpectedly gentle touch on the soft flesh below her navel.

'You're not cold like this, are you?' His voice was a husky undertone.

Suzy shook her head. The momentary apprehension had gone, dispelled by the lightness of his hold on her. She pressed closer, lifting her face to his, beginning to brush her fingertips over the nape of his long neck with the same small caressing movements he was applying to her spine.

They kissed, softly to begin with, then with increasing fervour. When her lips parted under his, she felt, between their locked bodies, a restless movement. But he went on kissing her mouth and stroking her back; making her more and more loving, more and more responsive.

By the time he picked her up in his arms, her mules falling off her feet as he swung her high against his chest, she was weak and dizzy with desire.

Her eyes closed, her head on his shoulder, she felt him stride through to the bedroom and lower her on to the bed. He must have flung back the bedclothes before joining her in the sitting-room. She could feel only smooth, starched linen under her back and legs. After the warmth at the fireside the sheet felt cool but not unpleasant. She stretched out, relaxing her thighs, her arms ready to embrace him.

When she felt his hand lift her ankle and his mouth on the sole of her foot, she drew in a breath of surprise at the tingle that shot up her leg. Where before, on her first night with him, he had merely caressed her with his hands, now he searched her body with his mouth, kissing her here, there and everywhere, driving her wild with pleasure.

Presently, trying a caress which made her spine arch, her fingers claw at the sheet, he murmured questioningly, 'Not nice?'

'Heavenly ... *heavenly*!' She couldn't begin to express the bliss which was rippling through every nerve in her body.

Wolfe repeated it, making her groan, 'Oh, God—no! No, no—I can't bear it!'

But he seemed to know that what she really meant was that she couldn't bear him to stop. He didn't. On and on, for what seemed like hours, he made her writhe, gasp and tremble as his warm, sure, experienced hands claimed their right to explore every inch of her.

At last, when there wasn't a sensitive place from the lobes of her ears down to the backs of her knees which had escaped his attention, and she had lost count of the times her body had shuddered with ecstasy, she felt his hard thighs between hers.

This time it was even wilder than in his bathroom in New York.

Afterwards, exhausted, she fell asleep, still in his arms.

She was woken by the murmur of voices—men's voices, speaking German. For some moments she couldn't think where she was, then she remembered and, listening, recognised Wolfe's voice but not that of the man who answered him.

The clink of china and silver made her realise he must be a room service waiter. Was it morning already? But if so, why was no light filtering round the edges of the bedroom curtains? And why was it lamplight not daylight which came through the slightly open door to the sitting-room?

Slipping out of bed, she went to the bathroom where she had left her watch. It was fifteen minutes past midnight. Wolfe must have woken up, felt hungry and decided to order something to eat.

What Suzy wanted was a shower. After bundling her hair into a cap, she spent three or four minutes standing under a jet of warm water.

When, sarong-wrapped in a bath towel, she wandered into the sitting-room—having first made sure the waiter was no longer there—she found Wolfe sitting by the fire, drinking coffee and eating a sandwich.

At the sight of her, he rose. 'I heard the shower running when I looked in on you a few minutes ago. Do you feel better for your sleep?'

Remembering what had caused her to fall into such a deep slumber at an hour of day—by her body-clock—when normally she would have been wide awake, the colour in her cheeks deepened.

'Yes, thank you. Didn't you sleep?'

He shook his head. 'I had some calls to make, including one to my grandmother. She was very pleased by my news and wants us to visit her when we leave here. Would you like some coffee?'

'Yes, please.'

Seeing that he intended to pour it out for her, she curled up in one of the armchairs, her bare feet tucked up beside her.

She wondered who else he had called. Madame Dupont? Lady Belinda? Surely he wouldn't allow either of his former mistresses to learn of his marriage from the Press. As yet no journalists knew that his bachelor days were at an end. But it couldn't be long before the news leaked out, and then it was sure to make a lead story, at least in the tabloids. It was just the kind of story they relished.

She could imagine the headlines.

Tycoon's Secret Wedding. Secretary Susan Snares Boss. Inevitably papers which ran a story of that kind would try to get quotes from the women she had supplanted. It was the least he could do to let Jacqueline and Belinda know what had happened before they were besieged by reporters seeking their reactions.

Nevertheless it hurt her to think of him talking to them while she lay sleeping in the next room.

'I ordered sandwiches, but perhaps you'd like something different,' he said, bringing a cup of coffee to her. 'Room Service goes on until one a.m. What would you like them to send up?'

'I'm not really very hungry. I'll have one of your sandwiches, if I may?'

He brought her a plate and a napkin, and the silver-plated, linen-lined tray of elegant, crustless brown and white sandwiches filled with smoked salmon, breast of chicken and his favourite cream cheese with chopped dates.

'What did your grandmother say?' she asked. 'Wasn't she astonished?'

'She didn't seem to be. Perhaps she had the perspicacity to see at once what I took some time to recognise; that my perfect secretary would also make a perfect wife,' he added with a gallant inclination of his head.

The compliment should have pleased her. Somehow

it didn't. She felt it had the ring of flattery rather than sincerity.

'She may not have expressed her amazement, but I'm sure she must have felt it,' she answered. 'I hope she won't be too upset. It can't be what she had hoped for.'

'She's too wise a woman to have hoped for anything but that I should be satisfied with my choice—which I am,' he replied, a trace of impatience in his tone.

The slight hint of irritability made her wonder if telling his grandmother had been a breeze compared with telling the other two.

She didn't think that Belinda, bred in the stiff upper lip tradition, would have made a fuss; but Madame Dupont might. She was a more volatile type, capable of making a scene. Not that Wolfe would have allowed her to rant at him for long. He would simply have cut the connection. But he would have to be extraordinarily callous for the upbraidings of a discarded mistress to leave him completely unmoved.

'You're frowning,' he told her. 'A bride isn't supposed to frown on her honeymoon. Not unless her husband's prowess as a lover has proved disappointing. I hope that isn't the reason you're looking pensive.'

'You know it isn't.' Avoiding his eyes, Suzy added, 'It was everything and more than I expected. It was . . . ecstasy.'

'In that case——' he strolled over to sit on the arm of her chair, '—why don't we do it again?'

Before she could answer he had loosened the towel she was wrapped in and was pulling it away from the warm, powdered curves of her bosom. Taking her gently by the hair, he pulled her head back and kissed her uplifted mouth, his other hand slowly caressing her shoulders and breasts.

Soon they were stretched on the rug, warmed by the replenished fire. And, as long as she was in his arms, his past and her future with him were erased from her mind by the overwhelming bliss of the present.

In the morning Wolfe went for his usual run before breakfast. He left Suzy in bed. But the moment he had gone she jumped out, brushed her teeth, pulled a comb through her hair and wriggled into her new banana yellow track suit. She had guessed that he wouldn't change his habits merely because he was on his honeymoon, and she intended to surprise him.

Although she had never jogged with him before nor, on a regular basis, by herself, she knew she was in excellent condition. The first course of exercise classes which he had inspired her to take had been followed by others. She had tried everything from aerobic dancing to yoga and exercises with Nautilus machines.

Keeping fit, begun as a discipline, had become a rewarding pastime she could practise wherever she went in their *mouvementé* life.

As she learned later, the *schloss* took its name from the beautiful lake, the Fuschlsee, which it overlooked. It was also surrounded by a magnificent park in which, presently, she met Wolfe returning from his run.

'What a glorious morning,' she greeted him, jogging on the spot as he approached her, ready to turn and run back to the castle alongside him.

He grinned, his teeth very white, his tanned features filmed with sweat.

'That's a very chic running outfit, but if you've run as far as this you might be wise to walk back,' he said, slowing his pace. 'I don't want a bride who can't move her thighs without wincing.'

Suzy laughed. 'Don't worry: I shan't seize up.' She kept going at his earlier pace.

She knew it would be some time before she could run at this speed for as long as he could. But her own daily bedroom work-out kept her muscles limber enough to stand a good deal of running without becoming painfully stiff. Because women lacked the testosterone hormone which governed muscle development, her fitness wasn't as visible as his. But she was no longer the feeble creature she had been when she started working for him.

Not far from the castle, she challenged him, 'Race you to that tree!' and started running flat out.

Even with her short start, she knew he would beat her. He did, reaching the tree several metres ahead of her and turning, his arms outstretched, as she came to the end of her sprint and flung herself at him.

Most men would have reeled under the impact. Not Wolfe. He caught her and held her as she panted for breath, inhaling deeply himself.

It was then, looking up at him with bright eyes and glowing cheeks, that she felt an almost overwhelming longing to say, *I love* you, and to hear him say, *I love you, too*.

But she couldn't say those words to a man who thought love was romantic nonsense.

'Now I'm famished,' she said, breaking free. 'What sort of breakfasts do they serve in Austria?'

'Big ones. But first you'd better spend ten minutes soaking in the tub. All this unaccustomed exercise could make you mighty stiff if you cool down too quickly.'

'Whatever you say. You're the expert.'

He hurried her inside the castle and up to their suite, where he ran a deep bath for her.

While she lay in it, she watched him shaving, admiring the play of muscle on his back as he used his razor to scrape away lather and stubble from around the firm lips which last night had given her such exquisite pleasure.

The only part of his body which lacked the all-year-round tan maintained by regular trips to such places as Acapulco and Tobago was the part covered by his bathing slip. Now, as he stood with his back to her, naked, she noticed that even his untanned areas were not as pale as her own natural skin tone.

When he had finished shaving, he went into the shower. She could see him through the glass door vigorously lathering himself, and hear him humming. It seemed a good omen for him to be singing in the shower on the morning after their wedding night. But at the moment she had novelty value. How long would that last? Would he still be humming in the morning after they had been sleeping together for a month . . . six months . . . a year?

When he came out of the shower, she stood up in the bath and opened the wastepipe. 'I think I'll wash my hair in there.'

She stepped on to the bath mat, trying to behave as unselfconsciously in front of Wolfe as obviously he was in front of her. At the moment, although her inhibitions soon disappeared when he started making love to her, when he was watching without touching she still felt a little shy with him.

During the time she had spent travelling with him, she had learnt that several medium-size toilet bags were more practical than one large one. She had a bag for manicure equipment and nail varnishes, a bag for her portable dryer and everything to do with hair, a third bag for medical necessities and a fourth for miscellaneous items.

It took her only a moment to find her tube of shampoo. As she moved past him to enter the shower, he caught her by the waist, pressing his mouth to the junction of her neck and shoulder, one palm sliding upwards to cradle a breast, the other hand moving downwards to the triangle of tight, wet curls.

'Shall I wash it for you?' he suggested.

His thumb was tracing slow circles on the smooth ring of rose-coloured skin surrounding the centre of her breast. His other hand was locating an even more sensitive spot. Suzy closed her eyes, starting to shake.

'If you like.' Her voice was unsteady.

Each time he did these things to her, her responses were quicker and stronger. If this went on, in a week . . .

He continued playing for a minute, then pushed her into the shower.

'In Singapore it rains like this.'

He turned on a lukewarm deluge which beat on their heads and shoulders as he took her in his arms and kissed her.

Later, after washing her hair with surprising efficiency, he spread towels on the floor and made love to her.

'The bathroom floor seems to be your favourite place,' she said teasingly, later on, while she was using her nail file to change the voltage selector on her dryer from America's 110 to Europe's 220.

'I prefer the floor to most beds, unless they have a board under the mattress. Making love well calls for a firmer surface than the average bed.'

She found his reply rather chilling; suggesting that what they had just done had been, for him, more akin to a particularly pleasurable form of callisthenics than to the emotional experience it had been for her.

After a leisurely breakfast, the Rolls-Royce took them to Salzburg, dropping them in a square dominated by a statue of Mozart, the city's most famous son.

Suzy quickly fell under the spell of the narrow streets lined with tall, centuries-old houses, the florid baroque architecture of the public buildings, the beautifully kept public gardens adorned with classical statues, and the glimpses of the mediaeval Hohensalzburg Fortress on its wooded hilltop.

'For almost a thousand years, this city was governed by Catholic bishops—although they behaved more like princes, 'Wolfe told her. 'The Mirabell Castle was built by one bishop for his mistress.'

It was a passing remark which anyone, knowing Salzburg's history, might have made. Coming from her husband, it was a painful reminder of his own princely disregard for conventions which, even in these modern times, still governed the lives of people like her parents and sisters.

The main shopping street was the traffic-free Getreidegasse, most of the premises having an ornate gilded wrought-iron sign indicating the wares within.

Wolfe insisted on buying her a dirndl, the charming national dress consisting of a tight bodice and full skirt worn over a pretty white blouse, often with the addition of an apron.

The one which he picked out for her was deep shocking pink patterned with a tiny white motif, with a fine lawn blouse frilled at the elbows, and a crisp white embroidered apron.

She would have liked him to buy one of the Junker jackets with contrasting lapels and silver buttons which many local men wore, but he laughed and declined. Leaving the dirndl to be collected later, he took her across the street to have lunch at the Goldener Hirsch, which he said meant the golden stag.

Inside the inn dark beams, white walls decorated with many stags' horns, painted chests and very old carved wooden chairs combined to give it the atmosphere of a private hunting lodge.

While they were having a drink in the bar where the barman had at once recognised Wolfe and welcomed him back, a man wearing the leather shorts called *lederhosen*, with dark stockings and a vivid pink tie and brown Junker jacket, came in.

He, too, recognised her husband. When the two men had shaken hands, Wolfe introduced him as Count Walderdorff whose parents had opened the hotel shortly after the Second World War.

'This is my wife, Johannes. We were married in New York yesterday morning. But please keep that to yourself for the present.'

Suzy remembered reading somewhere that most Austrian aristocrats were men of outstanding charm. As the director of the Goldener Hirsch gave her a courtly *Handküss* and expressed disappointment that she was not gracing his establishment, she felt that the statement held true in his case.

Later, having lunch in the domed dining-room where seats were booked eight months ahead for the white tie dinners after the Festival performances, Wolfe assured her there was no question of Count Walderdorff betraying his confidence.

'He's protected the privacy of far more newsworthy people than you and I. Royalty ... Presidents ... most of the richest and most famous people in the world have stayed here,' he told her.

He talked of the world-class musicians who used the inn as a club during the Festival—Herbert von Karajan, the Salzburg-born, internationally renowned conductor, singers such as Placido Domingo and Kiri te Kanawa.

Listening to his anecdotes about them, Suzy again found herself wondering who had been with him on those occasions. It didn't seem at all likely he had come to the Festivals alone. Were there bedrooms here where he had made love to her predecessors? Was that why he had booked a suite at the castle instead of at the Goldener Hirsch?

Such thoughts spoiled her appetite for the *Kalbsnieren-Braten*; roast veal boned and stuffed with a mousse of veal kidneys, garnished with watercress and game chips and served with a *Risi-Pisi*, a mixture of rice and green peas.

This was followed by *Salzburger Nockeln*, a marvellous confection of whipped egg whites and sugar enriched with yolks, vanilla and citrus peel and piled in mounds, or *nockeln*, on to a base of melted butter, thick cream and honey. This had been baked in an oven and, when it was brought to their table, the waiter poured a ladleful of flaming rum over it.

Wolfe had a second helping and tried to persuade her to join him.

'You can afford to put on a few pounds,' he said, eyeing her slender shape.

'If I do, the dirndl will have to be let out to fit me,' she answered lightly.

His remark left her wondering if it had been merely a pleasantry, or a hint that he preferred more voluptuous curves than she possessed. She didn't want to put on weight, but if it would please him . . .

After lunch they did some more shopping.

The ground floor of Mozart's birthplace was now a *Blumen Stube* or flower shop. As they stood looking up at the building, Wolfe said, 'He was three when he started to play the piano and twelve when he wrote his first opera. When he died, midway through his thirties, he left six hundred musical works—nearly all of the finest quality. And yet he was never well off, and often very poor.'

'Did he marry?' she asked.

'Yes: much to his father's annoyance, he married at twenty-six, a year after leaving home and going to Vienna. His wife, Constanze, was also a musician, but she added to his financial problems.'

'Perhaps they didn't mind being poor as long as they had each other and their music,' Suzy suggested.

Wolfe reaction to this was a sardonic laugh. 'Love

doesn't fill a man's belly, or keep him warm—except in bed.'

She forced herself to say lightly, 'No, I should think a good fire was rather essential in the winter in Vienna.'

Although her intellect could accept the validity of his remark, it served to underline, yet again, the limitations of their relationship. No other bridegroom, on his honeymoon, would have capped her romantic comment with that coldly realistic reply.

In another shop selling beautiful bouquets of dried flowers, they were told that this craft had originated in Austrian convents where the nuns had sought ways to decorate their chapels in winter.

The centrepiece of a shop devoted to herbs was an old sleigh laden with cotton bags of wild herbs gathered by countrywomen. One of the smallest yet most enticing of the city's shops was the Franz Raudaschl cheese shop; so tiny that there was room for only two or three customers to make their selection from more than a hundred different kinds of cheese.

Eventually, after buying several hand-painted boxes and decorated candles at the Heimatwerk shop specialising in local handcrafts, they strolled back to the square where the hotel's Rolls-Royce was waiting to take them back to the castle.

There, Wolfe suggested a swim in the indoor pool, after which they had tea in the sun on their balcony overlooking the lake.

'Now I think you should rest before dinner,' he said, smiling at her.

Which meant, of course, that he wanted to make love to her again.

For six days Suzy lived a life devoted to the pleasures of the flesh. The weather remained warm and sunny and they jogged together every morning before eating a hearty breakfast.

Later they went to Salzburg where, at mid-morning, they would emulate the Austrians for whom *Kaffee mit Schlag*—short for *Schlagobers*, a lavish dollop of whipped cream—was an essential part of the day.

Of all the *Konditorei* in the city, they liked best the oldest one, the Café Tomaselli in the Alter Markt, founded in 1703, with its oil paintings, dark wood panelling, chandeliers and small marble tables.

As well as offering many different kinds of *Kaffee* such as *Kleiner Brauner*, a small cup of strong coffee with a dash of milk, or *Teeschale Licht*, a large cup of milk with a little coffee in it, the Tomaselli had a wonderful selection of cakes. They included rich, bitter-chocolate *Sachertorte* named after the famous hotel in Vienna and *Linzertorte* with a lattice of hazelnut pastry.

Some of the local people seemed to sit in the café for hours, chatting to their cronies or reading the selection of newspapers and magazines provided for customers' use.

One morning Wolfe took Suzy up to the Café Winkler on the top of the Mönchsberg Hill with a wonderful view of the city and a wall-painting called the Sattler Panorama which enabled visitors to compare present-day Salzburg with the city as it had been in 1828. But the Winkler lacked the elegant comfort of the Tomaselli.

After coffee, they would explore the old city or look for presents for her family. This was his idea. He seemed to like shopping, and invariably picked out something to buy for her.

In the afternoon they went for long walks in the beautiful Austrian countryside. One evening they had dinner at Plomberg, said to be the country's finest restaurant, in the town which took its name from the Mondsee lake. Otherwise they dined at the *schloss*,

which had a choice of three restaurants, including a
romantic *wintergarden*.

And at all hours of the day and night Wolfe taught
her more about making love, making her realise how
basic her knowledge had been. But the verbal
expressions of love—the pet names, the private code
words, the secret language which people who loved
each other invented—were non-existent where she and
Wolfe were concerned.

He praised her appearance when she was dressed for
dinner. He said complimentary things about her hair.
But he never let slip the word darling, or any other
tender substitutes for Susan.

She wished that, just once, before he heard the
diminutive used by her family, he would call her
Suzy or Sue. His continued use of her full name
seemed to accentuate the lack of true harmony
between them.

For six days they were together almost every minute
of the day and night; and for much of that time they
were as physically close as two human beings could be,
even breathing the air from each other's lungs.

Yet, at the end of those days, they were still, in
many ways, strangers who knew nothing of each
other's innermost thoughts and deepest feelings.

The services of the hotel included Telex. Wolfe
received a number of messages, but he didn't show
them to her, saying that for the time being she needn't
concern herself with his business life.

On the morning of their seventh day at Schloss
Fuschl, he announced that he had to fly to London.

'There's no point in your coming with me. If I can't
get back tonight, I'll be here before lunch tomorrow.
You can use the time to recharge your batteries, as
they say,' he told her, with a quizzical gleam.

She had opted out of jogging that morning, pleading
exhaustion after being woken by caresses which,

within minutes of her awakening, had brought her to a shuddering climax—not once but several times.

He didn't say why it was necessary to interrupt their honeymoon, and she hesitated to ask. He hadn't told her how long they were staying in Austria and she hadn't asked him that either. Probably it depended on when he began to be bored by their sybaritic life.

She saw him off at Salzburg airport and then spent the morning in the city. After lunch, she tried the hotel's sauna and had a massage, her first.

It was not until she was alone in their suite, with nothing to do but listen to music on the radio or write messages on the picture postcards she had bought, that the thoughts she had been keeping at bay refused to be ignored any longer.

Had her husband gone to London to break the news of his marriage to the aristocratic Englishwoman whose name had for long been linked with his?

Had they lunched together? Had Belinda hidden her anguish with a brave face, making him feel grateful towards her for taking it so well? Grateful and also regretful that a long and pleasant liaison had to come to an end; and, if Wolfe found himself regretting having to end it, might he not, being a law unto himself, decide that it needn't be terminated—not if she were willing to continue it.

Pacing the luxurious private sitting-room in an agony of jealous conjecture, Suzy felt sure that no woman who loved Wolfe would be capable of refusing any means of keeping him in her life.

She herself had agreed to be his wife, knowing that he didn't love her. Would Belinda be stronger? All the evidence was against it. If she hadn't jibbed at sharing him with Jacqueline and Dena Sawyer, why should she object to sharing him with Suzy?

Maybe at this very moment they were in bed at his suite at the Connaught—if not there, at some other hotel. *He* hadn't been tired this morning. He was never tired. Making love twice in a day wouldn't tax his virility. He had made love to her twice a day ever since their arrival, sometimes more often. A change of partner was probably a fillip.

Hating herself for entertaining such horrible suspicions, but unable to dismiss them as impossible, Suzy continued to wander restlessly about until a maid came to draw the curtains and turn down the bed.

More for something to pass the time than because she felt hungry, Suzy rang Room Service—all the staff seemed to speak English or French—and ordered a light supper and, as an afterthought, a bottle of the Dom Ruinart champagne they had drunk with their dinner the night before.

By the time it arrived she was wishing she had asked for a bottle of Apollinaris mineral water instead. She wondered what the waiter was thinking as he unfastened the wire securing the cork: if his bland expression masked disapproval.

Then she realised that worrying about other people's opinion of her actions was a small-town attitude of mind which would irritate Wolfe if he knew of it. Her parents might think she was on the road to ruin if they could see her supper table, but the waiter was used to people who, if they happened to fancy it, would order caviar for breakfast and Mimosas at mid-morning. She must make an effort to cultivate a more worldly outlook befitting her new role as Mrs Wolfe Vyner, wife of an international financier.

Mrs Walker, the sedate young widow from Yorkshire, no longer existed. Her second marriage had made her a citizen of the world like her husband and, as such, she must cure herself of a lingering tendency towards provincialism.

The first glass of champagne stimulated her appetite. She had ordered chilled avocado soup followed by scrambled eggs *en croûte* with truffles, and *Gurkensalat*, a salad of sliced cucumber dressed with garlic, oil and white wine vinegar.

Her second glass began to dull the nagging ache of wondering what Wolfe was doing.

She had asked for a pot of coffee. It seemed that for once the hotel's impeccable service had slipped until, within a few minutes of her finishing the last delicious mouthful of flaky pastry, there was a tap at the door and the waiter reappeared.

'Perhaps madame would like to have her coffee by the fire?' he suggested.

'Yes . . . thank you. That would be nice.'

She rose and moved to one of the sofas. He placed the coffee tray on the end table. Then, having put her glass and the ice bucket within reach, he folded the starched damask cloth over the débris of her meal, let down the table's flaps and wheeled it from the room, bidding her a quiet goodnight before closing the door.

On the coffee tray there was a dish of some of the tempting handmade chocolates she had seen on sale in Salzburg. She poured a cup of coffee, added cream, and sampled a melting confection of black chocolate filled with fruit fondant and a liqueur.

She had eaten two more of the chocolates and was half way through her third glass of champagne when the telephone rang. The sitting-room extension was on the table beside the other sofa. As she crossed the fur rug, she realised that she was slightly woozy. The liqueur in the chocolates, even though there was only a thimbleful in each one, must be more potent than she had realised.

'Hello?'

'Are you lonely without me?'

'Wolfe!' She hadn't expected him to call her and the sound of his voice made her heart leap.

'What are you doing?'

'I . . . I've just had supper and I'm sitting by the fire eating chocolates.' She hesitated a moment before asking, 'What are you doing?'

'I'm drinking cognac and watching someone else eat chocolates. I bought her a large box of her favourite candied ginger centres at Charbonnel and Walker this afternoon. She'd like to speak to you.'

Charbonnel and Walker was one of London's best chocolate shops. Suzy wondered wildly if the voice she was about to hear would be Belinda Stratton's cool drawl.

'My dear, I am so very happy that Wolfe has at last found his life's partner. I was beginning to fear he would never find someone to suit him. But now all is well. I can look forward to being a great-grandmother before I depart from this world.'

For some seconds the relief was so great that Suzy was tonguetied. Fortunately it wasn't necessary for her to say much. After chatting to her for several minutes, the elderly Frenchwoman handed over to Wolfe.

'As you'll have realised, I couldn't make the last flight from London to Salzburg, so I thought I'd spend the night in Paris. I'll be back about noon,' he told her.

'Oh . . . good. Until tomorrow, then. Thank you for calling. Goodnight, Wolfe.'

He said, in French, 'Sleep well, my lovely one.'

But even as she replaced the receiver the happiness of hearing his voice and the unmistakable warmth of his grandmother's reaction to their marriage was spoiled by the thought that although Belinda might have failed to keep him in London, a night in Jacqueline's bed might be a greater temptation.

One of the things his grandmother had not remarked on was the fact of his deserting his bride in mid-honeymoon. Had she thought it was business which was the reason for this default, she would undoubtedly have made some tart comment intended for his ears rather than Suzy's. But obviously, with her knowledge of the world in general, and of her grandson's errant ways in particular, she must suspect that the reason was that there were others beside herself who had to be informed before his marriage was made public.

Suzy finished the champagne in bed. Combined with five liqueur chocolates, it sent her to sleep almost as soon as she lay down.

The following morning she felt ghastly, which seemed to disprove the myth that champagne never caused a hangover. Unless it was the rich chocolate which had disturbed her system, giving her a headache and making her feel queasy at the thought of breakfast.

A shower didn't make her feel much better. Before resorting to pain relievers, she ordered coffee and toast. She had to be back on form before Wolfe returned. A wan face might inspire tender sympathy in a man in love, but not in her husband.

She drank the coffee black, and ate the toast without the unsalted farm butter and black cherry jam she had enjoyed with it on previous mornings.

Presently, becoming conscious of a slight ache low down in her body, she realised her malaise was not solely the result of last night's excess of alcohol.

With so much else on her mind, she had forgotten the date. Realising that in spite of the emotional upheavals of the past three weeks, her body was maintaining its routine, she gave a groan of disappointment.

Now not only would Wolfe have to abstain from making love for a few days, but he might begin to wish he hadn't rushed into marriage quite so precipitately. She had an idea that he had expected her to become pregnant immediately; as, indeed, she had herself.

After breakfast she walked in the grounds and the fresh air and exercise made her feel almost normal.

When, soon after midday, the Rolls-Royce glided to a halt in front of the main entrance, she was waiting to greet her husband, wearing a flattering outfit which he hadn't seen before and a cheerful, welcome-back smile.

As usual he had travelled without luggage other than a briefcase. He returned with the distinctive black and gold plastic bag of his London booksellers.

'I thought you might like the latest English bestsellers and the English glossies,' he said, after he had kissed her cheek.

'Yes, I should ... how lovely ... thank you. Was your trip successful?' she asked, as they entered the castle. Not to ask might have seemed rather odd.

'Yes. A nuisance, but a necessary one. I think tonight we might let our hair down in a beer garden. Or doesn't that appeal?'

The swift change of subject didn't escape her. 'I like to try everything once,' she said, with forced lightness.

'Good—because there are several things we haven't tried yet.'

They were on their way up the staircase, out of earshot of anyone else, and the smiling glance which he slanted at her made it clear that he wasn't referring to local tourist attractions.

'Are there?' She couldn't imagine what. He had already introduced her to variations and subtleties she hadn't known about before.

When they reached their sitting-room, he hung the *Do Not Disturb* sign on the outer door knob, closed the door and locked it.

Dropping his briefcase and the bag of books on a chair, he held out his arms. 'Now we can say hello properly.'

She took a step towards him, then stopped. One thing she did know—Alix had told her—was that most women were less kissable than usual at the wrong time of the month.

'I'm afraid I'm . . . *hors de combat* at the moment.'

She wouldn't have expected him to be dense, but nevertheless it was a relief when he said casually, 'In that case perhaps you'd rather postpone the beer garden experience and spend this evening tucked up with one of the books I've brought you.'

It was precisely what she longed to do, but she said, 'No, no . . . I'm not feeling off colour. I'd love to go out tonight.'

Wolfe strolled across to the telephone. 'We'll see how we feel later on. At the moment, I'd like an appetiser.'

When she heard him ordering champagne, she wondered if she ought to interrupt and tell him she didn't want any. But on second thoughts she kept silent, intending to spin out one glass while he drank the rest.

However, after the first two reluctant sips, she found the champagne didn't reactivate her headache or queasiness. In fact it seemed to complete her cure.

After lunch Wolfe suggested she browse through the glossy magazines while he went for the run he had missed in Paris that morning.

Why had he missed it? she wondered, after he had gone out.

Because of an extra-late night chez Madame Dupont? Because the astute Jacqueline had taken advantage of his early morning virility to keep him in bed with her until the last possible moment?

CHAPTER TEN

OH, God, I must stop thinking these things, Suzy told herself desperately. I must cut out this paranoiac and absolutely futile jealousy. He's here with me now—not with either of them. He could easily have made an excuse to spend another night away, but he didn't. A wife is always in a stronger position than a mistress—if she plays her cards right.

When he came in from his run, Wolfe had a shower. Then he picked up one of the half dozen books he had brought her from Hatchards and was soon engrossed.

Since by then it was clear that he found the book—a Dick Francis thriller—unputdownable, Suzy didn't demur when he repeated the suggestion that they should dine where they were.

Soon after dinner, when Wolfe had returned to the book, she took the opportunity to have a leisurely bath and attend to various grooming rituals which from now on must be accomplished at times when he was not around, or at least not likely to walk in on her.

Afterwards she returned to the sitting-room in her nightclothes and said, 'I'm going to do as you suggested and turn in early.'

He looked up. 'Would you like some hot chocolate or toddy or anything?'

She shook her head.

'If you're asleep when I come through, I'll try not to disturb you.' He resumed reading.

Propped up with her two pillows and the one of his which he never used, Suzy settled herself comfortably with the book she had started.

She read for about an hour, then threw out two of

the pillows, switched off the lamp and lay down. To avoid letting her mind wander in undesirable directions, she thought about the forthcoming visit to her family.

One moment she was standing in the doorway of a room in the Walkers' farmhouse ... the next she was sitting up in bed with Wolfe's arms round her, trembling with the horror of her nightmare.

'You were dreaming. It's over now.' He stroked her back, holding her close.

It must have been the light which had woken her; the apricot glow from the silk-shaded bedside lamp, so different from the winter afternoon light in that faraway room in Yorkshire where ...

Still disorientated, gripped by the dreadful, vivid images of the past, Suzy burst into tears.

Wolfe held her close, smoothing her hair, letting her cry, her face buried in his shoulder. When she was calmer, he took a handful of tissues from the box on the night table and put them into her hands.

He said, 'I'll be right back,' and went through to the sitting-room. He was still fully dressed and the lights were on in the other room. Perhaps he had been reading still and had heard her cry out in shock and terror.

She peered through her tear-wet lashes at her wristwatch, lying on the table. It was only a little after midnight.

He returned with a tray on which was a bottle of brandy, a soda syphon, one glass and a small ice tub. He poured some brandy into the glass, diluted it with soda and handed it to her. Then he sat on the side of the bed, holding her left hand in his while she sipped the spirit, its warmth and fire steadying her, but not as much as the reassuringly warm, live clasp of his long brown fingers.

When she trusted her voice not to quaver, she said,
'I'm sorry.'

'No need to apologise, my dear.'

He switched on the radio, tuning through two or
three stations to find one playing light, catchy music.
She knew he was doing all he could to dispel the
reality of her dream.

'I've finished my book. I'll come to bed now,' he
said.

He stood up and began to undress, asking her if
there had been any clothes in *Vogue* or *Harpers &
Queen* she would like to buy when in London. By the
time he went to the bathroom, she had relaxed.

After they had put out their lights, he turned her on
to her side and drew her against him, her shoulder-
blades to his chest. As always, he had come to bed
naked. Tonight Suzy was wearing her nightdress.

'Goodnight, Susan.' He brushed a light kiss on the
ridge of her shoulder.

'Goodnight.' Mentally she added *my love*.

At that moment, snug and secure, it was easy to
pretend he loved her.

Next morning they jogged together as usual.

During breakfast Wolfe startled her by asking,
'What was your bad dream about?'

Suzy had put it out of her mind. She was surprised
he should remind her. Not wishing to dwell on it, she
said, 'Oh . . . it was very confused. You know how
dreams are.'

He gave her a long intent look. 'You were calling for
your first husband.'

She stiffened, trying not to let the dream revivify.

When she said nothing, he asked, 'Do you dream
about him often?'

'No. No, I don't . . . hardly ever. I—I went to sleep
thinking about Yorkshire and I suppose that

triggered something in my subconscious. What are we going to do today?'

He looked out of the windows for some moments. Suddenly she had the impression he was bored and restless; an intuition confirmed when he said, 'Perhaps we should fly to Genoa and drive down to the boatyard. It's some time since I've been there.'

They had been married for three weeks when they arrived in Yorkshire to visit her family. By that time she was convinced that Wolfe regretted giving up his freedom.

He was at pains not to show it, but she had known him for too long not to guess there was something biting him. Almost every night he made love to her. But afterwards, instead of sleeping, he would wait until he thought she was asleep and then, taking care not to disturb her, rise from the bed and leave the room.

As he wasn't involved in any important business deals—indeed he seemed to have lost interest in that side of his life—she knew that whatever was on his mind must be a personal problem.

Sometimes she would glance up from the book she was reading—they both spent a lot of time reading—to find him watching her.

Whenever she caught him studying her, he would make a complimentary remark about the length of her eyelashes, or the darkness of her eyebrows in contrast to her naturally blonde hair.

But she sensed that he hadn't really been admiring her looks. The brooding expression in his eyes had not been suggestive of admiration but rather of dissatisfaction; as if he'd been wondering what had possessed him to choose her to bear his heirs for him.

It was the fact that she hadn't become pregnant immediately which irked him, she felt. Perhaps he was worried that, of all the young women he could have chosen to be his wife, he had settled for one who was going to have trouble conceiving, or might even be barren.

Her common sense told her that, if this was in his mind, he was being unreasonable, to say the least. But common sense couldn't stop her worrying. She dreaded having to tell him, for the second time, that in spite of his intensive efforts to sire his first son, he had failed.

Or rather she had failed. For that was how he would regard it. The possibility that the fault might lie with him wouldn't occur to him.

They travelled to Yorkshire by air, then by hired car from Leeds to Brockthorpe.

'It's some time since you last saw your family. Are you excited?' Wolfe asked her, when they were a few miles from her birthplace.

She murmured assent, but in fact apprehension was a more accurate term for her state of mind at that moment. She was worried that he wouldn't like them and would find the visit a bore and another reason for regretting his precipitate marriage. She knew that if he found them tedious, they would never guess it. But he might arrange for an urgent summons to London to put an end to his ennui.

They arrived at her parents' house to find the whole family assembled to greet them; her mother and sisters with their hair newly set, the men wearing suits— under protest, she guessed—and a gargantuan 'high tea' set out on the best tablecloth in the dining-room.

She had telephoned twice in the past week, both times urging her mother to let them arrive without fuss. But clearly Mrs Campbell could not have gone to more trouble for a visit from the Queen.

Had she been happy and relaxed, Suzy could have borne this ceremonial reception with good humour.

Being already under stress, she found it an intolerable strain to have to introduce her husband to all her relations at once.

It was his savoir-faire which eased the tension of the occasion. Within ten minutes of entering the house he had put them all at their ease. He seemed to know exactly the right thing to say to each one of them.

Nevertheless, after being alone with him for three weeks, living in luxurious suites which made her parents' house seem very cramped and crowded by comparison, by the time they had finished tea Suzy was longing to escape to somewhere quieter and more spacious.

There was a good country hotel a couple of miles outside Brockthorpe. In the first telephone conversation she had told her mother they would be spending the night there. But it seemed Mrs Campbell had disregarded this plan and instructed her husband to prepare their guest room for the newlyweds.

'But, Mother, we've booked at The Grange. Wolfe is too tall to sleep comfortably in an ordinary bed. In America they have queen-size and king-size beds,' Suzy protested, snatching at a reason to avoid sleeping in the not very comfortable guest room where every movement made the old-fashioned bed springs creak, and where any sound above a low murmur would be audible in her parents' room across the narrow landing.

To her dismay it was Wolfe who demolished this excuse by saying, 'I doubt if the beds at The Grange are any larger than the one here. We can easily ring up and cancel our reservation—if you're sure it's no trouble to put us up, Mrs Campbell.'

'No trouble at all. We've been looking forward to having you. We'd be hurt if you stayed anywhere else, wouldn't we, dear?' she appealed to her husband.

'Indeed we would. I'll help you bring in your

luggage,' her father offered, obviously expecting them to have several large suitcases.

In fact they had only two small ones. Suzy had left most of her trousseau, including her fur, at the Connaught.

Longing for a leisurely bath, a glass of champagne and a respite from her sisters' questions—to many of which, such as where they were going to set up home, she had no answer—she braced herself for a difficult evening.

Later, when her sisters and their husbands had taken their tired and starting-to-be-fractious children home, and the noise level dropped, she found it less of a strain.

However, not long after their departure her mother reminded Mr Campbell it would soon be time for supper.

'You're right, my dear. The roast is coming along nicely, but it's time I attended to the vegetables.'

The realisation that they were shortly to have another substantial meal on top of an enormous tea made Suzy say, 'Not too many potatoes for us, Dad. We don't eat as much as you do.'

Her mother said, 'You don't eat enough, by the looks of you. You're thinner every time I see you. Don't you think she's getting too thin, Wolfe?'

'Oh, Mother—for heaven's sake! We've already eaten enough pies and cakes to sink a battleship. Instead of lecturing me about putting on weight, you ought to be nagging the others to lose some. Helen looks like the side of a house!'

The words were no sooner uttered than she regretted them.

Looking wounded, her mother replied, 'Now that's not kind of you, Suzy. Helen may be a little on the plump side, but she can't help that. It's her nature and the way Bob likes her.'

In spite of regretting her previous remark, Suzy felt driven to say, 'I hope you're right, because at the rate she's going——'

At this point Wolfe intervened. 'Suzy may be slimmer than her sisters, Mrs Campbell, but you needn't worry about her health. She's very fit. She may have been plumper when she was younger but I think it's her nature to be slender—and it's the way I like her,' he added, with a smile.

To have him defend her and use, for the first time, the affectionate short form of her name, made her ready to burst into tears.

Needing time to steady her jangled nerves, she said, 'I think I'll go up and wash, and unpack our night things.'

She had been upstairs for some time and was firmly resolved to keep calm for the rest of the evening when she heard footsteps on the stairs. When Wolfe entered the bedroom, he was carrying a glass of the sweet sherry her mother drank on special occasions. Her father always had one glass of whisky after his evening meal, but the Campbells never drank wine with their meals and in their eyes champagne was strictly for wedding receptions and twenty-first birthday parties. They would be shocked if they knew how often she drank it nowadays.

'Dinner will be ready in twenty minutes,' he told her.

She took the glass from him. 'Thank you. The bathroom is next door if you want to wash your hands. I put your wet pack on the window ledge.'

'Thanks.' He sat down on the bed, which squeaked under his weight.

Suzy sipped the sherry, grimaced at its syrupy sweetness and put it aside.

'Did they offer you a drink?'

'Yes, but I didn't want one. Your father has

suggested taking me to a pub after we've eaten. He seems to be under the impression I've never been outside London. It's also to give you a chance for a heart-to-heart with your mother.'

'I don't want a heart-to-heart. I know it's a rotten thing to say, but I've nothing in common with her, or my sisters, any more. It's all right as long as we're talking about the past, but when it comes to the present or the future, we're almost speaking different languages. I don't belong in their world now . . . and I don't belong in yours either.'

Her voice cracked. Quickly she turned to look out of the window, the once-familiar view blurred by the tears she had managed to control in the sitting-room.

The springs squeaked again as he rose. A moment later Wolfe's hands were resting on her shoulders as he stood close behind her, looking over her head at the well-kept back garden.

'Is it the past which is upsetting you?' he asked quietly. 'Does coming here bring it all back? Does it break your heart to remember him?'

The last question was so unexpected that, her throat already tight with emotion, Suzy couldn't answer it immediately.

Before she could speak, he went on, 'We can't go on ignoring something which is crucial to our life together. When I suggested our marriage, I didn't realise you were still in love with your first husband . . . or that I was in love with you.'

She gasped and swung round to face him, her expression incredulous.

'W-what did you say?'

'I wasn't going to tell you. I thought it would add to your burden to feel that I wanted something which you couldn't give me. But I think we have to be straight with each other. We can't go on hiding our feelings. I know how you feel about Chris, and now you know how I feel about you. If we try, we can make it work. Marriages—very good marriages—have been built on less,' he said quietly.

She laid her hands on his chest. 'Oh, Wolfe ... darling Wolfe ... you're so wrong! I haven't been grieving for Chris. I never think of him now ... not even today, coming back here. All my thoughts are of you. My heart has been breaking for *you*.'

He gazed down at her uplifted face, and she saw the uncertainty in his eyes. Sliding her hands upwards until her arms were round his neck and her body pressed against his, she said softly, 'Hannah warned me not to fall in love with you, but I already had. From the first day we met, I knew there was no other man who could hold a candle to you. You're everything I admire and respect and value ... and as well as all that I find you terribly attractive! If that isn't love, I don't know what it is. Hasn't it ever struck you that I'm the kind of old-fashioned girl who wouldn't have gone to bed with you if I hadn't been crazy about you?'

'Yes, that thought did occur,' he agreed. 'Especially after I found out I was your first lover. Before that I wasn't sure what you did in your private life. I once saw you in a pavement café in Paris with Robert Marigny. I was passing in a taxi. I know I was damned annoyed that you were seeing him and, presumably, sleeping with him. But I didn't recognise my reaction for what it was—jealously. It wasn't until that night in Austria, when you woke up calling for Chris and weeping, that I knew I loved you. Oh, Suzy ... Suzy ...'

His strong arms tightened. His head bent. As she closed her eyes, his warm mouth came down upon hers in a long, hungry kiss.

Quite a long time later, when he had relaxed that first rib-cracking embrace and was gently stroking her hair as she stood with her head against his shoulder, she said, 'There's something I haven't told you because I try not to remember it. Chris didn't die of his injuries. He . . . he took his own life. He did it to spare me being tied to someone who would always need nursing and could never be a father . . . or a husband, in the fullest sense. That night in Austria, I'd been dreaming about the day it happened. We were living with his parents then. They'd gone away for the weekend. His mother needed a break. She'd taken it terribly hard, as you can imagine. Her only son . . . crippled for life. I went for a walk with his dog. When I came back it was . . . too late. The worst of it was that after a while, when the first awful shock had worn off, what I felt was . . . relief.'

'That was a natural reaction. You mustn't feel guilty about it. You were much too young to be married at all,' Wolfe said gently. 'Marriage is for grown-up people, and no one is grown-up at nineteen.'

'I know. Later on I blamed my parents for not trying to make me wait. Legally, of course, they had no power to prevent us marrying, but they could have exerted some influence. Unfortunately my mother thinks that marriage is the be-all and end-all of existence for women. So do I—now. But there are other options. It makes sense to try some of the others before settling for this one'—lifting her face to be kissed again.

A few days later, in London, coming out of James Drew where she had been buying a silk shirt, Suzy encountered Belinda Stratton about to enter the shop.

By then Suzy was in no doubt that her husband's passion for her excluded any possibility of his continuing old liaisons or forming new ones.

Sustained by that happy certainty, she was able to say serenely, 'Hello. How are you?'

'Oh ... Susan ... good morning.' It was Lady Belinda who looked disconcerted.

And visibly unhappy, thought Suzy, with a twinge of compassion for her. Enveloped in the golden aura of being loved by the man she loved, she found it easy to pity the woman who had lost him.

They exchanged a few civil remarks and then parted, Suzy to stroll through the Burlington Arcade on her way back to lunch at their hotel.

Wolfe was already there. At one time she wouldn't have mentioned bumping into Belinda, but now there were no longer any areas of secrecy between them. It would have seemed unnatural and devious not to mention the meeting.

'Yes, I ran into her as well, on my way back from Christie's. If you're not busy this afternoon, they have a couple of sculptures I'd like you to look at.'

He went on to tell her about them, his encounter with Belinda dismissed with a casual lack of interest which, not long ago, she would have thought was assumed.

Now her trust was complete and unshakeable.

She went through to the bedroom to try on her new silk shirt.

Wolfe followed her. 'Perhaps rather than looking at sculptures we should be thinking about somewhere permanent to house them. The first question to settle is where to set up home first—here, in America or in France.'

'I don't mind. Wherever you prefer.'

She finished unbuttoning the shirt she had worn to go shopping and cast it aside. Instead of shaking out her new one, she went to him and put her arms round him.

'Home for me means right here,' she said, as she snuggled against him.

A WORD ABOUT THE AUTHOR

Although Anne Weale and her husband are British, they have lived for the past five years in a Spanish villa perched on a clifftop above the Costa Blanca – Spain's beautiful "white coast." From her desk in a corner of the drawing room she enjoys a wide view of miles of Mediterranean coastline.

Anne and her husband are world travelers, and recent destinations have included Florida, New England, Italy and the Caribbean. A constant companion is Anne's portable typewriter. More than once she has been tempted to start tapping the keys in the middle of the night!

Actually, Anne feels a book is improved if there is time to mull over the first flash of inspiration for a few weeks before putting it to paper. Also, there is usually a great deal of background reading to be done, as well as on-the-spot research. This involves talking to as many of the local inhabitants as possible, spending hours in the local-history section of the library and generally seeing everything there is to be seen.

Anne's husband is an invaluable help to her with her writing. She explains that his viewpoint coincides with the hero's. While she disappears downtown to explore the shops, he may head for some historic fortification. His impressions and observations of his excursions have found their place in many of her novels.

Anne Weale began her writing career as a journalist but gave up journalism to follow her husband to the Far East. Out of her first two years of living in an exotic land came *Winter Is Past* (Romance #582), set in Malaysia–the first of more than fifty books by this favorite Harlequin author.

Yours FREE, with a home subscription to SUPERROMANCE™

Now you never have to miss reading the newest SUPERROMANCES... because they'll be delivered right to your door.

Start with your **FREE** LOVE BEYOND DESIRE. You'll be enthralled by this powerful love story... from the moment Robin meets the dark, handsome Carlos and finds herself involved in the jealousies, bitterness and secret passions of the Lopez family. Where her own forbidden love threatens to shatter her life.

Your **FREE** LOVE BEYOND DESIRE is only the beginning. A subscription to SUPERROMANCE lets you look forward to a long love affair. Month after month, you'll receive four love stories of heroic dimension. Novels that will involve you in spellbinding intrigue, forbidden love and fiery passions.

You'll begin this series of sensuous, exciting contemporary novels... written by some of the top romance novelists of the day... with four every month.

And this big value... each novel, almost 400 pages of compelling reading... is yours for only $2.50 a book. Hours of entertainment every month for so little. Far less than a first-run movie or pay-TV. Newly published novels, with beautifully illustrated covers, filled with page after page of delicious escape into a world of romantic love... delivered right to your home.

Begin a long love affair with

SUPERROMANCE.

Accept LOVE BEYOND DESIRE **FREE.**

Complete and mail the coupon below today!

- -

FREE! Mail to: SUPERROMANCE

In the U.S.
2504 West Southern Avenue
Tempe, AZ 85282

In Canada
649 Ontario St.
Stratford, Ontario N5A 6W2

YES, please send me FREE and without any obligation, my
SUPERROMANCE novel, LOVE BEYOND DESIRE. If you do not hear
from me after I have examined my FREE book, please send me the
4 new **SUPERROMANCE** books every month as soon as they come
off the press. I understand that I will be billed only $2.50 for each book
(total $10.00). There are no shipping and handling or any other hidden
charges. There is no minimum number of books that I have to
purchase. In fact, I may cancel this arrangement at any time.
LOVE BEYOND DESIRE is mine to keep as a FREE gift, even if
I do not buy any additional books.

NAME _____ (Please Print)

ADDRESS _____ APT. NO.

CITY _____

STATE/PROV. _____ ZIP/POSTAL CODE

SIGNATURE (If under 18, parent or guardian must sign.)

SUP-SUB

This offer is limited to one order per household and not valid to present
subscribers. Prices subject to change without notice.

Offer expires August 31, 1984   134 BPS KAK